CW01551658

STEVE PEMBERTON

THE ACCIDENTAL DRAGONRIDER

Books by
Steven J Pemberton

The Barefoot Healer (fantasy)

Death & Magic
Plague & Poison
Dust & Water
Stone & Silence

The Schemes of Raltarn & Tomaz (fantasy)

The Mirrors of Elangir
The Dragons of Asdanund (forthcoming)

The Dragonrider Series (fantasy)

The Accidental Dragonrider
The Reluctant Dragonrider

Other Works

Escape Velocity (science fiction)
Simon and the Birthday Wish (for children)

Chapter 1

A great rush of air from above knocked Iko to the ground. A shadow blotted out the sun. As the wind subsided, he became aware of a hulking presence in front of him, heavy beyond mere physical mass. Expecting it to be the last thing he ever did, he looked up.

The tip of the dragon's nose was about three feet in front of him. Its head and body were covered in jet black scales. Its eyes were the palest gold, with a narrow vertical slit in the middle, black as the bottom of the ocean, seeming deep enough to contain worlds.

The dragon shifted its weight slightly, and its nostrils dilated. Air moved past Iko as it breathed in. This was it, then. How long might it be before someone noticed he was missing? If they came up here to look for him, would they work out the meaning of the blackened patch of grass where he now lay?

Man-thing. The voice reverberated inside his skull. The legends were right: dragons had no voices like humans, but spoke directly with their minds. What the legends hadn't mentioned was that the dragon's mindspeech was incredibly loud. Perhaps he should move further away? Given his present circumstances, that might not be a wise move.

Crawling, said the dragon. *Grovelling, as befits your kind. Were you another dragon, I should kill you for this insult. Yet one such as you is scarcely worth that trouble.*

The dragon paused and breathed out. Iko's head rceled as if from blows. The ground seemed to spin underneath him. Still, he had survived a lot longer than he had expected to after the dragon's arrival. At the moment, he wasn't sure whether that was a good thing. Carefully and distinctly, he framed words in his mind.

O great dragon, he said, *I offer my most humble apologies for disturbing you.*

It speaks! The dragon seemed quite startled. Its pupils widened fractionally.

Iko hadn't been sure his mindspeech would work, so that was a relief. Would the dragon hear everything he thought? No, his sources said that you had to want your thoughts to be audible. *O great dragon,* Iko said, *I have made some study of the ways of your kind, but there is, of course, much of which I am still ignorant. I assure you that I mean no offence. I would be most grateful to learn the correct manner of addressing you.*

Polite, too. There was an uncomfortable pause. He imagined that the dragons had never had to consider such a question, at least not when it was being asked by a human. *"O great dragon" will suffice,* it said eventually.

Perhaps, o great dragon, you wish to know why I summoned you here.

You did not summon me, said the dragon, and Iko sensed anger behind the words. *I chose to come.*

As you wish, o great dragon. Iko bowed his head.

Look at me, said the dragon, and Iko complied. He knew that he couldn't have disobeyed. *I am nevertheless curious to know why a man-thing happens to be on this hilltop, far from its own kind, at the very same moment that I choose to visit it.*

That is quite simple to explain, o great dragon. I wish to propose an alliance.

An alliance? To what end?

O great dragon, a fleet of pirates are preying on the people of the Lenis Islands, attacking our settlements and ships. We are a peaceful people, not used to fighting —

And you wish me to destroy these... pirates for you, said the dragon.

Yes! Remembering his manners, he added, *Please.*

You would have me burn their ships with my fiery breath? Capsize them with a sweep of my tail? Pluck man-things from the sea and carry them aloft, shrieking, before I flip them into my mouth to crush them and swallow them whole?

He winced at the dragon's suggestions. *I had thought, o great dragon, that the mere sight of you would terrify them into leaving us alone.*

Perhaps. And what do you offer me in return for ridding you of these vermin?

The pirates have a great horde of treasure on their ships and in their home port — gold, silver, precious jewels. If you defeat them, it is yours.

The dragon did not reply. The corners of its mouth lifted, revealing glistening white teeth. Its nostrils narrowed, and a sound like a tree falling filled Iko's mind. *You know far more of our ways than I would have expected of any man-thing. But there is much of which you are ignorant.*

A gale rushed past him, pelting him with dust and twigs. By the time he could see again, the dragon was no more than a spot in the sky, an odd-shaped bird spiralling upwards. Almost at the limit of sight, there was a violet flash, and the dragon was gone. Iko brushed the worst of the dirt off his clothing and started the long walk back to the village.

What now? This outcome had never occurred to him. He hadn't seriously expected the summoning to work, but had thought that if it did, the dragon would most likely kill him immediately for his impertinence. He imagined the taunts of the children, the pitying looks of the monks and the other teachers. *Typical Iko. Can't get anything right.* He decided to say nothing about it. If anyone asked where he'd been, he'd simply climbed the hill to admire the view. Stretch his legs. Clear his head.

He saw no one on the road that led into the village from Samdurath, the next settlement along the coast. That wasn't so unusual, but when he saw no one in the main street, nor any of the side streets that intersected it, he began to worry. He jogged the rest of the way to the house that he still shared with his mother.

The door stood open. Smoke hung in the air — the fire had gone out. A half-eaten meal lay at one end of the table. Guilt tugged at him as he noticed the place she'd set for him at the other end. He didn't have any classes today — he should've come to have lunch with her, not chase after creatures of legend that didn't care what happened to decent people.

"Mother!" he shouted.

No answer came. He opened the door to the bedroom. She wasn't there. Sweating, he squeezed between her bed and the linen chest to reach the back door. She wasn't in the garden either.

Iko tried to calm himself. She must have gone visiting. But why leave her lunch unfinished? Realisation crept up on him. Not only had he not seen anyone on the way here, he hadn't heard anyone. The pirates had attacked while he was away. Everyone was dead or taken captive.

His knees gave way, and he fell to the ground. Tears fought for release. Was this why the dragon had refused to help? Because it knew he was already too late?

He forced himself to stand. If Mother's fire was still smouldering, they couldn't have gone far. He scrambled through the house and ran for the harbour. He couldn't do anything for his own people, but if he could see which way the pirates were going, he might be able to warn whichever village they were heading to next.

The two jetties were intact, with boats moored at both of them. Nets, crab traps and coils of rope lay neatly next to each boat, as if everybody had gone to the tavern to share a few bottles of wine. One boat still had a couple of buckets of fish next to it. No vessels were visible at sea.

Panting, Iko tried to make sense of the scene. The pirates' ships were too big to moor in the gaps between the villagers' boats. If they'd used the jetties, they would've cut some of the boats loose and made a mess of the villagers' fishing equipment. If the ships had stayed further out and lowered boats of their own, there should be keel tracks and footprints on the beach, which there weren't. Now that he thought of it, he'd seen no sign of a struggle anywhere in the village. More than that, he'd seen no dead or dying people. The pirates couldn't have taken everyone — some of the villagers would have put up a fight, and the pirates would have killed them.

Not daring to hope, he turned and ran back inland. The

people must have seen the pirates coming and taken refuge in the monastery. They could stay safe for weeks there. But then why had the pirates not ransacked the rest of the village?

As he turned the corner onto the long approach to the monastery, he saw that the gate was closed. His heart leapt — it was always open except in the presence of an immediate threat. He sprinted the last hundred yards and rattled the bars.

"Hey! It's Iko! The pirates have gone!" Through the gaps in the bars, he saw that the courtyard was deserted. "Open up!" Shouldn't there be men with swords and spears waiting there? Or at least a couple of lookouts?

A young man peered around the edge of the gateway. Startled, he gawked at Iko before saying to someone behind him, "Yes, it's him."

Relieved to see someone alive, Iko grabbed the bars for support.

"Figures," said an older man. "I suppose you'd better let him in." Iko recognised the voice of one of his mother's cousins, though he couldn't recall the man's name. The younger man was his son or nephew, who'd passed through Iko's classes a few years ago without much learning settling on him. He went back behind the wall and started to turn the wheel that operated the bar that held the gate shut.

"It's all right," said Iko, raising his voice over the squeaks and scrapes of the gate swinging open, "the pirates have gone. The village is empty."

"Pirates?" said the older man, coming into view. "As if we haven't got enough to worry about with a bloody great dragon flying around the place."

Staring at him, Iko almost forget to let go of the gate when it swung open. "Yes. Of course. Dragon. Big. Black. Flying. I... I believe I can explain that."

Chapter 2

Iko hesitated outside the Proctor's door. He wanted to slink off and hide somewhere far away.

You've faced a dragon, he told himself. *How could the Proctor be any worse?*

Uninvited, another part of his brain replied, *If the dragon had decided to kill you, it would've just got on with it. It wouldn't have lectured you about your failings first.* He lifted his fist and knocked.

"Come in!" called the Proctor.

The Proctor's office was as Iko remembered it from the few times he'd been in here — large, dimly-lit and filled from floor to ceiling with books that held the details of every pupil, teacher and monk who had passed through the monastery since its founding. An especially large example of one of these lay open in front of the Proctor, and Iko wondered how much of it was filled with his record.

The Proctor closed the book and looked up. He seemed to have aged since Iko saw him yesterday. "Teacher Iko," he said. The formality was a bad sign — not that Iko had expected him to be friendly. "No doubt you've heard the reports of a... large flying creature being seen over Ansrad Hill earlier today."

Iko opened his mouth to speak. A croak came out. He swallowed and tried again. "I have, Sir." Although the hill itself couldn't be seen from the village, it was visible from the monastery's towers, and from out at sea. And of course, anyone could have seen the dragon arriving or leaving.

"These reports caused the villagers to panic and take refuge in the monastery. Do you know why they did that?"

"The creature was a dragon, Sir."

The Proctor glowered at him. "Some of the villagers said it was a dragon."

Iko took a step back. "Do you not believe them, Sir?"

"What I believe is irrelevant. What matters is that the people are afraid of another pirate attack. If we stand united against the pirates, we can repel them. That will not happen if the people are constantly looking over their shoulders, anticipating fiery death from the skies."

"I suppose not, Sir."

"Which is why you will say nothing to anyone about this alleged dragon. If anyone asks, you saw nothing. Teacher Tenuha will gather descriptions from eyewitnesses and then announce that the creature was a bird, most likely an albatross. The people will laugh at themselves for being so credulous, and within a week, the incident will have been forgotten." He tapped the book, as if to say, *Except by the records.*

Iko licked his lips. "It was a dragon, Sir. I was on the hill when it landed."

The Proctor gave him a look that could have nailed him to the wall. "You. Saw. Nothing."

Bowing his head, Iko mumbled, "Yes, Sir."

"You are dismissed."

That night, Iko lay awake in his bed. Mother had scolded him for not heeding the call to take refuge in the monastery, but hadn't been curious about what he'd been doing instead. She'd been swept up in the general panic, and hadn't heard the rumours about the dragon — or if she had, didn't believe them.

What now? All that time in the archives figuring out how to summon a dragon, the spell had worked first time, and he had nothing to show for it. He didn't doubt that the Proctor would expel him if he told anyone else the truth. Eventually, he sank into sleep, no nearer to any answers.

Man-thing. Return to the hilltop.

Iko jerked awake, sweating. Dark shapes resolved themselves into the walls and door of the bedroom, and Mother asleep in the other bed. Of course. He'd dreamt of the dragon — the alleged, imaginary dragon — and had heard the voice of its

9

mind in his. Dawn wasn't far off, so he might as well get up.

He considered heading to the monastery for breakfast, but decided to wait for Mother to wake so he could tell her where he was going. She slept a lot more nowadays, though that was to be expected — she was getting on for fifty. He busied himself with chores, and then sat on the porch, watching the sunrise until Mother called his name.

There was no conversation as they ate. As he was about to leave, she said, "Make sure you stay at the monastery until it's time to come home."

He had classes for most of the day, so it shouldn't be hard to comply with her request. "I will."

She threw her arms around him and leaned up to kiss his cheek. Awkwardly, he returned the embrace. She hadn't done that since Father died, almost five years ago. He patted her shoulder and eased out of her arms.

"Take care," she whispered.

He shambled through the morning's classes, repeating himself and mixing up material from different subjects. Towards the end of the history lesson, he caught himself about to declare that the Third War of the Nuhysean Succession had been caused by Lord Brahan's inability to solve quadratic equations. Worse, he doubted that any of his pupils would have queried it — they were as shaken as he was after yesterday's panic.

A few days later, while Iko was eating luncheon in the monastery's refectory, one of the permanent monks, a dumpy, genial woman called Drubath, approached him and asked, "Teacher, might I have a word once you've finished your meal?"

Iko nodded and hurried through the rest of his food. He had been one of the referees for the thesis that got Drubath her permanent status, an analysis of one of the crucial battles of the Asdanundish War. He'd worked with her a few times since, helping her locate citations for monographs on various aspects of Nuhysean culture and history around the time of the war. As he approached her table, she stood up and indicated that they should go outside.

The courtyard was less occupied than he'd have expected at

this time of day. Drubath glanced around, perhaps checking for eavesdroppers. As they walked, she said in a low voice, "I'm curious about the... creature that frightened everyone a few days ago."

Iko stopped as his stomach lurched. "I — I'm sorry, Sister. I can't help you. I didn't see anything."

Drubath turned to face him, one eyebrow raised. Had his denial been too swift? Too glib? Someone must've noticed he'd been spending a lot of time in sections of the archives that weren't related to any of his classes.

She stuffed her hands into the pockets of her robe. "I didn't say you did see anything. It's more of a... hypothetical question."

"Oh. Carry on, then."

They resumed walking, and Drubath said, "I've heard... some of the villagers..." She glanced at him sidelong. "I know this sounds ridiculous, but they're saying it was a dragon."

He snorted, even as his throat went dry. "Ridiculous, yes."

"I know. It's been at least four hundred years since the last documented sighting. There was one about fifty years after that, over Untashekh, but the dragon was at quite a high altitude and only two people saw it..." She tailed off as she realised Iko was staring at her.

"I'm sorry, Sister," he said, dropping his gaze. "You're not seriously saying you believe dragons actually exist?" *Kashalbe, I must sound so false.*

"I did say it was a hypothetical question. They existed at some time in the past. I'm not sure whether they still do."

"Sister, I'll thank you not to repeat such nonsense. It could cast grave doubts on your academic credibility."

She stood straighter. "Our histories and legends are full of them. They were instrumental in our victory at the Battle of Karn Ridge."

"A battle that occurred a thousand and twenty-four years ago, and which may have taken place fifty miles from the geographical feature it's named for. Anyway, I thought you wanted to talk about whatever frightened the villagers into taking refuge the other day."

"I do." She fidgeted with something in a pocket.

"Then why are you talking about dragons?"

"Because — hypothetically — if the creature was a dragon, somebody must have summoned it here."

Iko glanced around. That wasn't how the dragon had seen it. "You cannot summon something that does not exist."

"All sources agree on that point," said Drubath. "Dragons are not of this world, and can come to it from their home only at the request of a human. When the alarm bell rang, everybody who was in the village came into the monastery before we shut the gates. Everybody except you, Teacher."

"You don't seriously think I — summoned this — hypothetical — no, this non-existent dragon?"

She gave him a knowing smile. "I didn't say that. But nobody I've spoken to mentioned seeing you while they were coming to the monastery. So where were you during the alarm?"

"Is there a point to this line of questioning?" Was she intent on blackmail? Teachers weren't rich enough to be worth the bother. Or had the Proctor told her to test his obedience?

"It occurred to me that if this hypothetical person who hypothetically summoned this hypothetical dragon was hypothetically planning to summon it again, there's certain knowledge in the archives he might benefit from." She took something from her pocket and pressed it into his hand. It was a scrap of paper with a short sequence of letters and digits — the classmark of a book in the archives. He didn't recognise the section code at first, and had to think where it would be.

"This is Elangic philosophy," he said. "Third millennium. What's that got to do with…"

"Misfiled."

"Oh." He'd thought he'd read everything the archives had about dragons. He put the paper into his own pocket. "Well, Sister, if — hypothetically — I was the hypothetical person who summoned the hypothetical dragon, I would have to thank you — hypothetically."

Drubath tilted her head. "And if you're not that hypothetical person?"

"Then I thank you for drawing my attention to this misfiled book. I'll see that it's put in the proper place and the catalogue amended."

"I'm always glad to help, Teacher. Good day." She turned and walked back towards the main building.

Chapter 3

Iko waited a few days before checking Drubath's book. He wasn't sure he wanted to know what it said. His dreams of the dragon continued. Always the creature wanted him to return to the hilltop where he had summoned it — or where it had chosen to appear.

Eventually, after classes, he went to the south-west annex, where they kept works relating to Elangir and the islands of the Tian Ocean. The top-level classification of the archives was geographical, although there was little consistency as to whether a work was filed according to the nationality of the author or the place he had written about. The annex was bright and airy by the monastery's standards. Everything was much more spread out, possibly because they hadn't acquired nearly as many Elangic works as the founders seemed to have expected. Iko made a show of consulting the catalogue and wrote down a few classmarks near to Drubath's.

When he reached the right place among the shelves, he found that the work was not a book, but a scroll. He unrolled it a few inches. Sure enough, the title was *Some Notes Concerning Dragons*. Trying not to whoop with joy, he picked up a few others and took them to a reading desk.

The scroll was written in Middle Nuhysean, and so had to be at least eight hundred years old. The text started without preamble, not even stating the name of the author. He puzzled his way through it. Most of the words he knew, and could guess the rest from context, but some of the spellings were strange. That meant the scroll was older than most of the documents he'd read. The text generally agreed with what he already knew, but about a quarter of the way in, he read —

The colour of a dragon's hide is generally a reliable indicator of its age, insofar as they are white when they hatch and gradually darken with age. They assume many colours over the course of their lives, but the oldest are invariably black. They become capable of mating on their second change of colour, and the females generally lay one clutch of eggs with each such change. Changes happen between thirty and fifty years apart. Once a dragon becomes black, it can no longer mate.

That was why the dragon had spurned his offer of the pirates' treasure. There were several theories as to why dragons hoarded treasure, but the most popular was that they used it to attract a mate. If that was the case, gold and jewels would hold no appeal for a black dragon. So what could he offer the dragon to persuade it to frighten the pirates away — or destroy them, if that was what it took? Or could he summon a younger one?

"Unusual to see you in here, Iko."

The Proctor stood in front of him. Praying that he wouldn't ask why the scroll was in Middle Nuhysean instead of Elangic, Iko licked his lips and replied, "One of my pupils this morning asked a question I couldn't answer."

"I admire your dedication," the Proctor said with a smile, "if not your preparedness." He walked on.

Iko held his breath as the Proctor's footsteps passed out of earshot. He returned to the scroll. A foot or so further down, he read —

Some claim it possible to bargain with a dragon to persuade it to perform some task or service, in a manner like unto the demons of Perakhandra. But whereas a demon will act in strict accordance with the letter of the agreement, exploiting any hole or ambiguity in its wording, a dragon will do whatever the summoner lacks the strength to prevent it doing. Dragons are adept in discerning what a man values most and taking it from him. This is why dragons hoard treasure — not because they have any use for it, but to twist a knife in a man's guts.

Iko was sceptical of the existence of demons, which inclined him to disregard the contents of the scroll. Then again, if

15

someone had asked him last week whether he believed in the existence of dragons, he might well have said no.

He slept little that night. Visions of the dragon kept him awake. Instead of burning the pirates' ships and harbour, it laid waste the village because of some inadvertent insult he had given it. The stones of the monastery held out a while longer before the beast's fire melted them.

Man-thing. Return to the hilltop. Now.

Sweating, Iko sat up. Moonlight from the window bathed the scene, giving everything an unreal appearance. He hadn't imagined the dragon's voice in his mind. It had come back to Ansrad Hill and was waiting for him. Why? It regarded humans as vermin. If it wanted to kill him, it would be no extra bother to level his house — or the entire village. But perhaps the creature had some sort of honour. It had no quarrel with anyone else here. If he went to meet it, perhaps it would spare the rest of the population.

Moving carefully, so as not to wake Mother, he got out of bed, gathered his clothes and went into the main room, where he dressed. Outside, the night was unseasonably cool, with few clouds. He had perhaps three hours before the moon set — plenty of time to reach the hill and — assuming the dragon deigned to let him live — come back.

When he reached the bottom of the hill, he squinted at the top, trying to pick out the dragon. He saw no sign of it, and it hadn't spoken to him since he left home. He trudged to the top and stood in the spot where he had met the dragon, or as near as he could tell — everything looked different in the moonlight.

Still there was no evidence of the dragon. There was nowhere hereabouts it could have been hiding — even with its wings folded, it was bigger than his house. Maybe he'd just dreamt it wanted him to come here. He paced around, kicking at pebbles, wondering whether to go home.

Man-thing. Run!

Startled, Iko stopped and looked around. Still there was no sign of the dragon — though if its mental voice could carry as far as the village, it could be anywhere.

Leave the hilltop! Now!

He wasn't about to argue with a creature the size of a building. He ran back the way he'd come. A gust of wind slapped him from behind. He tripped and rolled several yards before slamming against a boulder. Something large and heavy landed behind him, making the ground shake. Pieces of grit and gravel struck the exposed areas of his skin.

Man-thing. Are you there? The dragon's voice sounded much weaker than before.

Spitting out dirt, Iko levered himself upright and thought through what he wanted to say. *I am here, o great dragon.* Wincing, he climbed back to the top of the hill. The dragon lay there, stretched out, smoke and steam rising from it. Its eyes were closed, and one of its front legs was bent under its body at a painful angle.

Gods preserve us, Iko whispered. *Are — are you hurt?*

One eyelid flickered. *Your Gods do not watch over us. And I have survived worse.*

What happened?

I fell out of the sky.

That much seemed obvious. *Is there anything I can do to help, o great dragon?*

Next time I call you, answer right away, instead of waiting a week of your time.

I don't understand, o great dragon, Iko said. Something dark glistened on one of the teeth that protruded beyond the dragon's upper lip. The lack of colour made it hard to be sure, but he guessed it was blood. Seeing the dragon from the side for the first time, he realised he'd been wrong in thinking it was the size of his house. It was much bigger. Its head alone was too large to fit in the main room.

Is it my fault you... fell out of the sky? Iko asked. How was that possible?

That... and my fault for choosing to visit this place at the same time as you.

Forgive me, o great dragon. That was not my intent.

We may as well dispense with "o great dragon," the dragon said. *We will be in one another's acquaintance for some time to come. You may address me as Esald.*

17

Iko bowed, trying not to clench his teeth as his knee twinged. *Thank you, o... Esald. My name is Iko.*

I did not ask it. But perhaps you have earned the right to be called something a little more prestigious than "man-thing."

Thank you. Does this mean you agree to my proposal?

Esald's upper lip lifted an inch or two. *I did not say that.*

Then... what happens next?

Your kind rest at night, do they not?

Yes.

Then rest, Esald said. *Return here when I call. Immediately.*

It takes me an hour to walk here, said Iko.

That is acceptable. Now go.

What if I'm asleep?

My call will wake you.

You're hurt. Will you be all right?

Do not concern yourself with that. Go!

As you wish. Farewell. He bowed again, then turned and walked back down the hill, not daring to look behind him. Dragons, he recalled, were blessed with an extraordinary healing ability. Whatever was wrong with Esald would probably be fixed by morning.

The moon was setting as Iko got back to the village. A couple of fishermen were heading down the main street to the jetty, but he managed to avoid being seen. No one else was around, and he slipped back into the house and into bed.

Iko awoke to sounds of panic outside. In the distance, the alarm bell clanged. He jumped out of bed and shook Mother awake.

"What's going on?" she asked, yawning.

"I don't know," he replied, though he had a good idea. He looked out of the front door to see the neighbours hurrying along the street.

"To the monastery!" one of them shouted at him.

"Why?" he called at the man's retreating back.

"The dragon's returned," the man replied over his shoulder.

Iko swore under his breath and ducked back inside.

"What is it?" Mother asked.

He ran a hand through his hair. "We, ah, need to take

refuge in the monastery."

Mother frowned. "Again? Over a silly albatross?"

"Um, yes — that's probably all it is, but, ah, everyone else is going, and we wouldn't want them to worry about us, would we?"

Mother hobbled over to the cupboard and started putting items into a basket. A plan formed in Iko's mind. Prising the basket out of her hands, he said, "Let me do that — you go on ahead."

"Are you sure? It's dangerous for you to stay here on your own."

"If you're not frightened of an albatross, why should I be?" he said, standing aside and gesturing to the door. "I'll be right behind you." He couldn't recall the last time he'd lied to his mother, and he thought she would surely see through his deception.

But she nodded and crossed to the front door. On the threshold, she said, "Don't dawdle."

He continued putting things into the basket for another minute or two, then went to the door. Mother was already out of sight, so he handed the basket to the first person he saw and asked her to ensure that Mother received it. Without waiting for her to ask why, he went back through the house and climbed over the garden fence. He sprinted out of the village on the road towards Ansrad Hill. It wasn't until he had to slow down, panting and sweating, that he realised he was still wearing his night clothes.

He stopped and wiped his forehead. His legs ached. When had he last run that far or that fast? He reached out with his mind to try to talk to the dragon.

Esald, can you hear me? It's Iko. The villagers have seen you. I'm coming to the hilltop.

He waited for several heartbeats without an answer.

Esald, are you there?

Still no answer. He took a deep breath and resumed his journey at a fast walk.

As he clenched his teeth against the aches in his muscles, Iko ran through reasons why Esald would have come to the hill and not answered him. The dragon had said he would call for him, presumably when he was ready. He hadn't said anything about the possibility of Iko calling for him. Last night Esald had elevated him on his social scale to somewhere above cockroaches and midden worms, but he guessed that didn't mean it was now acceptable for him to drop in unannounced like an old friend. Perhaps his mental voice didn't reach as far as the hilltop — the dragon's thoughts had been much louder than his own. Perhaps the dragon was asleep. Did dragons sleep? Some of his sources claimed they slept when they were guarding treasure, but otherwise —

He turned a corner and could now see the hill, a couple of miles distant. The dragon lay at the top, not moving.

Esald!

Iko ran for the hill. He reached the base sooner than he would have thought possible and half-walked, half-stumbled to the summit. Esald lay where he had fallen the night before, eyes closed, muscles slack. The grass and bushes had withered, and the ground was dry and cracked, as though after a long drought.

Gasping, Iko limped over the hard, uneven dirt to the dragon's head and put a hand in front of one of Esald's nostrils, wide as a fencepost. He was still breathing, the air almost too slow to flutter a sail.

When had Iko started thinking of the dragon as *he* rather than *it?* When he learned the creature's name, probably, though he had no idea whether *Esald* was a masculine or feminine name.

Esald, can you hear me? No answer came. He placed a hand on the top of his snout. The scales felt like worn sandstone, cool to the touch. He saw now that they were not uniformly black: the smaller ones tended towards slate grey or dark purple. Three parallel grooves ran across the top of the snout and down one side — scars from a battle with another dragon? Behind his head, a wide bony crest rose, protecting the back of the neck. This had many long scratches, and one side of it looked as though it had been chewed.

The leg that had been under the dragon's body last night

now jutted out. The angle still looked painful, though he had no idea what sort of postures would hurt a dragon. Three toes as long as his forearm each ended in a talon the size of his outstretched hand. A dark patch on the ground under the foot caught his eye — blood? As he started to walk towards it, the dragon snorted and his head rolled towards him. He staggered out of the way and tripped, hitting the ground hard.

Iko opened his eyes, surprised to find himself lying down. He might stay here for a while. It was pleasantly cool, with a gentle breeze, and he needed a rest after all that running.

A noise came from behind him. He ignored it. The noise repeated. A moment later, something poked him between the shoulder blades. He rolled over, intent on swatting the disturbance away. The end of a wooden pole hovered a few inches from his face. His gaze followed the pole backwards to a nearby shrub.

"Iko!" a man whispered. This man, one of the villagers, was crouching behind the shrub and holding the pole.

Iko sat up and put a hand to his head to try to quell the sudden throbbing there. He blinked several times and squinted at the interloper, who had withdrawn the pole. "What are you doing here?"

The man shushed him and said, "Come over here. Slowly — we don't want to wake the dragon."

"He won't wake up," said Iko. "I've already tried."

"What? Look, just come over here."

Iko pushed himself upright and stood still for a moment to make sure of his balance. A dozen or more men lay on the ground behind the one who'd disturbed him. Most of them held spears or bows, pointed towards the dragon.

A sickly feeling formed in Iko's stomach. "What are you doing?"

The man behind the bush stepped away from it. Now at last Iko recognised him — Serl, the villagers' leader. He grabbed Iko's arm and dragged him behind the other men. He drew a sword and offered its hilt to Iko. "Either get back to the village or help us kill the monster."

"You can't do that," Iko said. He told himself the reason he hadn't known Serl right away was because the man had been leader for only a few months, not because he paid no attention to what was going on in the village. "It's — he's — injured."

"Then it should be easier to kill."

"No, no — there's no need to kill him — he's not dangerous."

Serl gawked at him. "Of course it's dangerous — it's a sodding dragon."

"I summoned him here," said Iko.

"Kashalbe's arse," Serl growled. "I always knew you lot were mad."

"I was hoping he'd help us defeat the pirates."

Serl's mouth hung open for a moment, and then he raised his spear. "Aim for the eyes, lads."

Iko darted in front of him and tried to knock the spear aside. Serl punched him, making him stagger backwards.

"Now!" Serl yelled. Bowstrings thrummed, and then arrows and spears clattered against the dragon's hide. "Again!" The men who'd thrown spears unshouldered bows, while those who'd started with bows fumbled to reload.

"No!" shouted Iko. He scrambled to his feet and ran towards the dragon. One arrow protruded from his nostril; the others had had no effect. An arrow whistled past Iko. He reached the dragon and put his arms across the crest behind the head.

"Get out of the way, you Gods-damned idiot!" Serl demanded.

"You can't kill him," Iko panted, turning to face the men. "He hasn't done any harm."

"If we wait for it to attack first, there won't be any of the village left for us to defend."

One of Esald's eyes opened.

"Oh Mazor, it's waking up," said Serl. "Get out of the way."

Esald, can you hear me? Iko thought. *These men have come here to kill you.*

"If you don't get out of the way, I won't be held responsible if you're hurt," said Serl. He pulled back the string of his bow. Several of the other men did the same.

Hold tight, said the dragon. *Do not let go until I tell you.* Iko

22

gripped the edge of the crest. A leathery rustling sound came from behind him.

"*Iko!*" Serl's hands trembled, and his eyes glistened.

Iko gave a sad smile and shook his head.

"Loose!"

Wind buffeted him, and his arms were jerked upwards, making him scream as his shoulders and elbows twisted. The dragon rolled and pitched as Iko fought to contain rising nausea. This was worse than any bout of seasickness. By the time he found the courage to look down, the hilltop seemed no bigger than a molehill. The men were almost too small to see.

Iko felt his hands slipping. Every joint in his arms burned. *Please, Esald, put me down. I can't hold on much longer.*

Just a little more altitude.

One of Iko's hands let go, and he swung around, hitting the dragon's shoulder. The leg came up to pin him against the dragon's body. There was a blinding flash all around him, and the pain was suddenly gone.

Chapter 4

Iko woke to find everything a uniform shade of pale purple. He wondered whether something was wrong with his eyes, but when blinking and shaking his head a few times didn't change the view, he decided it was real. A breeze ruffled his hair and clothing. He hung beneath Esald's chest, supported by the dragon's front feet. One talon was uncomfortably close to his neck. Its edge was pitted and cracked with age, but it looked more than sharp enough to slit his throat.

Esald? Where are we?

Patience, Iko. Do not move.

Iko shuddered and tried to relax. A sparkling below made him realise they were flying over an ocean. Apart from being purple, it looked just like the one he knew. A few patches of violet fluffiness hung a little way above it — clouds?

How high up are we?

I do not think you would like the answer to that question.

I wouldn't have asked if I didn't want to know.

Five verses. Perhaps six.

Verses?

There is a song called The Ballad of Rodan and Isme, *about the founders of our race, that we teach to dragons when they are white. We measure heights by counting how many verses of it we can sing while ascending or descending.*

I see, said Iko. It wouldn't be as accurate as a clock or trigonometry, but he supposed it didn't matter as long as you could tell when to pull up to avoid hitting the ground.

Iko heard a swoosh behind him, and Esald climbed several yards. He realised that Esald had been gliding, like an albatross — no wonder the Proctor had claimed that was what he was — and had flapped his wings, just once, to maintain height.

Something that had been niggling Iko came to the front of his mind. He squinted and scanned the horizon. Seeing nothing, he said to Esald, *I thought dragons couldn't fly out of sight of land.* It was the main reason why the first people who figured out how to ride dragons hadn't conquered the world with them.

In your world, we cannot.

Are we not in-in... my world any more, then?

Was it not obvious from the purple sky and the absence of a sun?

Iko had known that dragons inhabited their own world, but hadn't considered what that might mean in practice. When he'd given it any thought at all, he'd imagined the dragons' world as being like Asdanund or Perakhandra — remote, but somewhere he could visit in principle, and no different from the Lenis Islands in any fundamental way.

He looked around for a sun, not seeing one, though of course Esald's body blocked his view of most of the sky. *If there's no sun, where does the light come from?*

The sky, Esald replied, as if it was a stupid question.

They flew on for what felt like hours. Iko's ribs ached from pressing against the dragon's feet, and his neck had grown stiff from holding his head clear of the talon. An island came into view, tall and jagged, like a shard chipped from something much bigger. Against Iko's expectations, it was not purple, but grey, with patches of green on the slopes that were far enough from vertical to hold on to some soil.

I will be landing soon, said Esald. *I will have to throw you clear just before I touch the ground. Otherwise, I am liable to break my front legs.*

And crush me, Iko replied, his mouth suddenly dry.

I assumed that would be obvious. When I let go of you, make yourself into a ball so that you roll when you hit the ground. That will minimise the risk of serious injury.

The dragon began a slow, spiralling descent. Each time the island came into view, it seemed much closer than before.

When they came out of the spiral, they were heading for a ledge that looked barely wide enough for Iko, never mind Esald. Above it was a near-vertical rock face, hundreds of feet tall and wide.

You can't possibly land there! said Iko.

Be quiet, Esald replied.

Iko shook with fear. He tried to turn his head so that at least he wouldn't see the wall as they crashed into it, but it was too big for that. The dragon raised his head and neck and beat his wings once, twice, three times. The steady wind that had been pummelling Iko became turbulent, and the pressure of the dragon's feet on his body was gone. It took him a moment to realise the dragon had thrown him.

Roll, you fool! Esald shouted.

What was the point? He was about to hit a solid wall at a speed greater than any human had ever reached. Round or flat, it would make no difference to how dead he was.

He hit the wall.

His eyes burned with an intense flash of purple light.

He was still moving.

Some instinct told him that perhaps he should heed Esald's advice, and he started to bring his knees up to his chest and wrap his arms around his shins. Before he could complete this manoeuvre, his foot caught on something, and he went tumbling over and over, more and more of his body banging and scraping on the rough, hard ground. Eventually he came to a stop, face down, every part of him sore.

A gust of wind passed over him, and a series of loud, echoing clicks approached — the dragon's claws on the rock.

Iko? Esald sounded almost concerned. Iko lifted his head fractionally. *Iko, can you hear me?* The dragon nudged his flank, then rolled him over, prompting a whimper of pain. *Why did you delay in following my instructions?*

Iko raised his arm to examine it. He'd taken off a fair amount of skin, and beneath a tear in his sleeve was a good-sized cut, but that didn't look to be too deep. His elbow felt as though it had been twisted sideways, as did one of his knees. He touched his cheek, which stung, and his fingertips came away stained red.

"Why didn't you tell me," he began.

Esald interrupted with, *I cannot understand those noises you make by flapping your mouth.*

Iko took a deep breath. Something tickled the back of his throat and triggered a fit of coughing, amplifying his pains. When the coughing stopped, the pain subsided, leading him to guess — or hope — that he hadn't broken any bones.

I told you, said Esald, *I cannot understand those noises.*

"I wasn't —" *I wasn't trying to speak that time. Why didn't you tell me the rock wall was an illusion?*

The illusion — deceived you?

Obviously. Iko took a few moments to look around. He was in a cave, easily the size of the monastery's archives. The cave was longer than it was broad, and the roof formed a dome over it, so that the overall shape was of half an egg on its side. Soft purple light came from spherical crystals embedded in the ceiling and walls. Three tunnels led out of the chamber, one each to the left, the right and the back, all dragon-sized. The left-hand one was lit by more of the purple crystals, but the other two were dark.

A blanket of warm air from Esald's nostrils rolled over him. *Being bonded to me does not entitle you to address me as another dragon would.*

Bonded? Iko stood, cautiously, testing that each joint still worked. The dragon stood before him, wings folded, though the cave looked big enough to let him spread them without touching the walls. Behind him, in place of the wall Iko had thought they were going to hit, was a clear expanse of purple sky.

Esald tilted his head. *Do your books and scrolls not explain that concept?*

No. I read everything I could find in the archives about dragons, but I found nothing about "bonding."

No matter. It would almost certainly be wrong. Esald stood straighter, stretching his neck and legs and unfolding his wings about halfway. *I brought you here to show you something. Enter the lit tunnel and follow it to its end.*

Steven J Pemberton

Iko quivered as he obeyed. He told himself it was because he was shaken from the landing, not because he didn't trust Esald enough to turn his back on him. He almost believed it.

The tunnel curved slowly to the right, going deeper into the cliff. It became narrower and lower, to the point that Esald would have had to tuck his wings in. After a few dozen more yards, Iko wondered whether the dragon would've been able to pass at all. Now he noticed holes in the walls where crystals must have been, and claw marks on the floor, deeper and longer than those at the entrance. The tunnel grew still smaller, and Iko thought he might be able to touch the roof with his fingertips if he jumped. Then the tunnel widened again and opened into a room perhaps half the size of the one he'd just left. At the sides and back of the room, the floor rose in a series of broad shallow steps. Most of the floor was covered with glittering gems and small metal discs. Further back were statues of people and mythical beasts, and what looked like a metal tree.

Iko took a couple of steps into the room, then stopped when his foot brushed against something that clinked. He bent and picked up a few of the metal discs, one red, two purple. They all had a picture of a face in profile on one side and an animal on the other. Of course — they were coins, and the purple light had altered their colour, just as it had everything else. The language of their inscriptions indicated they were Asdanundish — over a thousand years old, if he'd read the dates correctly.

This was Esald's treasure hoard. He tried to estimate what it might be worth... more than every settlement in the Lenis Islands and everything in them. As many coins as he could fit into his pockets would make him the richest man in the village, several times over.

He didn't want to be rich: he wanted to be free from the fear of pirates. Besides, the legends said dragons were insanely jealous of their treasure, and would relentlessly pursue anyone who stole so much as a clipped penny. Was that why Esald had allowed him to see this — because he thought he wouldn't dare take anything? He put the coins back where his foot had kicked

28

them and returned to the main chamber.

Now do you understand why your pirates' treasure holds no appeal for me? Esald asked.

Yes. Yes, I suppose I do.

I must take you to a conclave of dragons.

Oh, said Iko. *Why?*

So that they can decide what to do with you.

I thought you'd already decided.

If the decision was mine alone, said Esald, *I would have let go of you a little earlier on the way here.*

Iko tried not to shudder. He had moved up from "man-thing" in the dragon's estimation, but was still a long way from being considered a friend. Did dragons even have friends?

But the decision is not mine alone, and you are not merely a stray wyvern.

Do wyverns exist, then? I thought they were just a story.

Esald half-closed his eyes and raised one side of his upper lip. *As dragons are "just a story?"* Iko guessed the facial expression was analogous to a human rolling his eyes. *Stand before the illusion.*

Why? said Iko.

So that I can pick you up.

I've no desire to repeat that experience.

Your desires are irrelevant.

But I might fall, or cut myself on your claws. Couldn't you... carry me on your neck or your back?

The dragon bared his teeth. *I am not a horse.*

Trembling, Iko stepped back. *I... I didn't mean to imply that you were, o-o great dragon.*

You are wasting time. Stand before the illusion.

Iko obeyed. He heard the dragon move around behind him and then charge. Before Iko could think about getting out of the way, something large and heavy struck the middle of his back, and he fell.

Chapter 5

Wind tore the breath from him. His clothes whipped his skin. He was going to die. Why had the dragon tossed him aside like a piece of rubbish? Was he not even worth the bother of killing with tooth and claw? The sea spread before him, too large to comprehend.

A shadow passed over him, then a great *whoomph* of air buffeted him. Esald's claws closed around his chest. The dragon flapped his wings twice, three times, and the dive flattened out. Iko shut his eyes and gulped down air. He thought he heard something skim the water. Esald had left one of Iko's arms free, and he used that hand to wipe some of his sweat away.

"What in the name of —" He stopped, recalling that the dragon didn't understand spoken language. *What in the name of all that's holy do you think you're doing?*

I need to run in order to gain enough speed to fly. And I cannot run with a man-thing between my front legs. The dragon beat his wings again, gaining height.

You took off from the hilltop without running, Iko replied.

That was an act of desperation. And I had the sky above me. Esald made a broad slow climbing turn, before heading out over the ocean. *I have not previously had to carry something as large as you that needed to be kept alive. Now that I can judge the times and distances better, I will catch you sooner the next time.*

Iko gulped. *I don't want there to be a next time.*

Nor do I. But the decision is neither mine nor yours. The dragon flapped his wings a few more times, then settled into a glide.

They flew on for what seemed like hours. Pinnacles of rock

occasionally came into view, none much closer than the horizon. Iko thought he saw a few other dragons, but couldn't be sure. Whenever Esald settled into a glide, Iko felt himself dozing off, but was woken by the upward jerk as the dragon flapped his wings. At least Iko was more comfortable this time — the dragon's toes interlocked, forming a basket for him to lie in, with the talons safely out of the way. Pressed against Esald's chest, he was also warmer than before.

There was no sun in the part of the sky he could see. He looked for variations in the sky's colour — it should be lighter near the sun and darker away from it — but saw none. The whole sky was a uniform mid-purple, as if it was a flat painted surface.

Twice he noticed disturbances in the ocean, just below the surface, too big and too uniform to be shoals of fish. The second time, he asked Esald what they were, and received the reply, *Nothing that need concern you.*

Eventually, Esald started circling, losing height. When he straightened out, he was heading for a large island, lower and flatter than the sharp peaks. As it drew nearer, Iko realised that some of the things he'd taken for rocks were other dragons, hunkered down.

We are nearing the place of the conclave, Esald said. *I will have to throw you again, but it should be a gentler landing than before. I will throw you to one side, so that I do not crush you.*

That would be one of the more embarrassing ways to die, Iko thought to himself.

As they neared the island, Esald reared upwards to hang almost motionless over a broad sandy beach. His front legs parted, and he flipped Iko to the right, giving him a slow spin. Before Iko had time to panic, he hit the sand, rolled twice, and came to a halt face up. He lay there panting, waiting to see if the urge to vomit would pass.

A shadow fell across him, and the dragon's head loomed over his face. *Stand. They are waiting for us.*

Iko obeyed, his body protesting a combination of soreness from the flight and sharp pains from the landing.

Inland, said Esald. *Do not speak unless I permit it.*

At the top of the beach, a narrow twisting path of hard-packed earth cut through waist-high grass. As he followed it, Iko wondered who — or what — had made it. He had seen no living creature here besides the dragons. Esald padded beside him, much less graceful on the ground than in the air. He bludgeoned the grass with his snout and front legs, leaving it looking as though a couple of elephants had charged through.

The ground slowly rose, and the grass became shorter and thinner. A couple of minutes after leaving the beach, they came to an open area of bare dusty grey rock, about the size of the monastery and its grounds. Around the edge, three dragons lay, crouching like cats ready to pounce on a mouse. Two were black like Esald, and even larger than him. The third, between them, and the smallest of the three, was wine red, a colour none of Iko's books had mentioned.

Esald, said one of the dragons — Iko couldn't tell which. *So you spoke truthfully about the vermin.*

When have I ever spoken untruthfully? Esald replied.

Never, to my knowledge. But it has been so long since a man-thing entered our realm that we found your assertion hard to believe.

The black dragon on the right stretched his neck and tilted his head. *Tell it to approach so that we can smell it.* The voice was different from the dragon that had spoken previously.

Iko started to take a pace towards the speaker, and then wondered if he was supposed to wait for Esald's instruction.

His name is Iko, said Esald, *and he understands our speech.*

All three dragons raised their heads, and the two black ones half-spread their wings.

A rider? said the dragon who had spoken first. *We should kill him now!*

I never said he was a rider, Esald replied. *I have told him my public name. You should do likewise.*

The black dragon on the left introduced himself as Kelekh, the red one as Athera, and the black one on the right as Vadim. From the mention of public names, Iko wondered if there were private names, and if so, whether knowing one would grant him power over the name's owner.

Does it speak? said Vadim.

Yes, said Esald. *Iko, say something.*

Iko lifted his chin and gazed straight at the dragon. Some of his sources said this was a challenge, but others said it merely showed the dragon you weren't afraid of him. Slowly and carefully, he formed the words in his mind. *Greetings, o great dragons. I thank you for allowing me into your presence.*

The dragon's mouth snapped shut. *Are you a rider?*

I am not, o great dragon. Humans have not ridden dragons for nearly a thousand years.

That is not such a long time to us.

He has none of the rider's tools, Esald said. *He spoke no words of command to me.*

Iko's sources had been vague on the subject of words of command, or at least on the subject of what words existed and what they meant. They were unambiguous about the drastic and usually fatal consequences of making a mistake with such words.

Then how did he bind you?

Esald did not answer. Iko wondered if the question was meant for him.

Speak, said Athera.

He did not bind me, Esald said, and Iko fancied he heard embarrassment in the dragon's voice. *He spoke the words of summoning, it is true, but I chose to enter the human realm.*

Why did you do that? said Kelekh.

Again, Esald did not reply immediately. *I had not thought any human would dare to speak them. I had intended to kill him for the insult — for the reminder of that dark time. But also, I was curious as to how a human could know the words and yet be so ignorant of elementary precautions in dealing with our kind.*

And what do you say to that, man-thing? said Vadim.

O great d-dragons, Iko replied, *when humans rode dragons, it was a small, privileged group who did this. Most of what they knew about you, they kept secret among themselves. Much of their knowledge died with them. The books I read to learn about your kind were written by people who were not riders. Some of them, I suspect, had never even seen a dragon.*

Typical human arrogance, said Vadim.

Athera said, *So if he is not a rider and he did not bind you, why did you bring him into our realm? And why have you troubled us with him? Are you so old and feeble that you cannot dispose of one human?* The two black dragons turned their heads towards Iko. From Vadim came a noise like a lion's growl, but much deeper.

I am bound to him, said Esald. *I did not say he bound me.*

I had not thought you one to speak in riddles, said Kelekh.

Iko tried not to show any surprise at that remark. Esald had done little else since he met him.

We have long known that binding was not just a matter of speaking the required words, said Esald. *Some humans could do it and some could not. Iko may have rider blood in him, several generations back. That, combined with the fact that I entered the realm willingly, may have allowed him to inadvertently bind me.*

Binding is never inadvertent, said Kelekh. *He must have had some ambition to control you, even if he did not know what would happen.*

He thought to bargain with me, said Esald.

Bargain? said Kelekh, in a tone that made Iko wonder if he knew what the word meant.

His clan is weak, and is under threat from a stronger clan. He asked me to destroy his enemies, in return for which I would take their treasure.

The dragons shook their heads and waggled their wings. Was this their version of laughter?

Not merely a riddler but a maker of tales, said Kelekh.

It is true, said Esald.

Have you forgotten how we fought to be free of obligation to humans? said Athera.

Have you forgotten how they enslaved us? said Vadim. *Forced us to fight in their petty, meaningless wars? Pitted sibling against sibling? Parent against child? They thought we were animals — too stupid to know any better!*

This was news to Iko. His sources had no definite answers as to why dragons were no longer to be found in the human realm.

I have not forgotten, said Esald. *Both my grandfathers died in the Liberation. I wanted to avenge them, but my father forbade me to fight.*

We have all heard that story many times, Esald, said Athera. *Do you still hunger for vengeance? Do you think that killing this human's enemies will grant it to you?*

Leave them to their squabbles, said Kelekh.

There are days when I still desire vengeance, said Esald. *But I know that killing this human's enemies will not grant it. No human alive remembers that time, or even understands it. For them, it is twenty generations past. Vengeance taken on someone who does not understand why it is taken is no vengeance at all.*

Twenty generations? said Kelekh. *Absurd!*

They do not live as long as we do, said Esald. *If you allow this one to come closer, you will smell the rot that emanates from him. He is already halfway between birth and death.*

At twenty-four, Iko thought, he was probably nearing the mid-point of his life, though it wasn't something he liked to think about.

We will take your word for it, said Athera.

Iko wondered why, if the dragons had been slaves of humans a couple of their generations ago, they didn't know how long humans lived. Unless they'd suppressed or forgotten any knowledge about humans that wasn't related to how much they hated them.

So, Esald, said Athera, *you have carelessly allowed yourself to become bound to a human, and you want to be unbound.*

Kill the human, said Vadim, almost before Athera had finished.

Iko tried to stand firm, reminding himself that death was no more than he'd expected from the moment he'd summoned Esald.

At his age, the backlash would kill him, said Kelekh.

Not if one of us does it, Vadim replied. *That was how we freed ourselves from the riders.*

I had not thought you held me in sufficient regard to endure pain on my behalf, Esald said.

Even if he did, said Athera, *I will not permit it.*

That was the first sign Iko had seen of a hierarchy among the dragons. He'd assumed Athera's smaller size and the fact he wasn't black meant he was junior to Kelekh and Vadim. He let out a breath, relieved that they weren't going to kill him — or weren't willing to accept the consequences of killing him.

Then what shall we do? said Esald.

No one spoke for a few moments. Iko licked his lips. They might think him rude, but what could they do about it? *May I make a suggestion, o great dragons?*

I told you not to speak unless spoken to, said Esald.

We may as well hear what it has to say, said Athera.

Am I right in thinking that this "binding" has come about because I used some magic?

Yes, replied Athera.

We know little about magic nowadays, Iko said, *but I have heard that anything that has been done by magic can be undone by magic.*

That is correct, said Athera.

Again, no one spoke for a moment.

Did you think we knew the spell? Esald asked. *If so, I would have used it at the earliest opportunity — and your bones would be black ash now.*

If it was so simple to undo a binding, said Kelekh, *the Liberation would not have been so costly.*

We would never have been enslaved in the first place, said Vadim.

I assume, said Athera, *that you do not know the spell either, man-thing.*

I do not, said Iko, rankling at how he had been demoted to "man-thing" again.

There is another possibility, said Kelekh. *The binding that the riders used was breakable only by death, and compelled the dragon to serve his rider. It took days, if not months, to complete, and was started when the dragon was young and less able to resist.*

What of it? asked Esald.

The binding that the man-thing used took a matter of moments, and although you are old, you are much stronger than the young dragons that the riders used to bind.

So you think the binding is weak?

Weak enough that we might not have to kill the man-thing to break it, said Kelekh.

How, then, said Esald, *if not with a spell of unbinding?*

Is the answer not obvious? said Kelekh.

Assume it is not, Esald growled.

The binding forces you to serve the man-thing. If it is weak, you might break it with a short term of service.

Serve? Never!

Assuming you do not wish to risk death, said Athera, *you appear to have no choice.*

Esald reared up on his back legs, flapped his wings, and let out a deafening roar. Panicked, Iko ran along the path that led to the beach. After a dozen paces, he tripped and sprawled on the earth. Spitting dirt, he rolled over and sat up, in time to see the other dragons shaking their heads and waggling their wings — laughing at him.

Clearly, said Vadim, *the man-thing will not be able to command much service from you.*

Removing an infestation of pigeons, perhaps, said Kelekh, *or digging a latrine trench.*

Whatever the service, said Athera, *I am certain you will perform it to the best of your ability.*

You may depend on it, Esald snarled.

There is one other small matter, said Athera, *although I am sure you have already considered it.*

I am sure I have, Esald replied, *but tell me anyway.*

For as long as you are bound to the man-thing, killing it or harming it, even accidentally, will have severe consequences for you. So perhaps it would be inadvisable to carry it in your front legs in flight. You might easily drop it or crush it whilst landing. Better, perhaps, to let it climb onto your back.

I am not a horse! screamed Esald.

We can see that, Athera replied. *But neither are you a dragon who would attempt to wriggle out of an obligation that — by your own admission — you willingly entered into.*

Esald let out another roar, not as loud as the first. He flapped his wings a few times, then lowered his head.

Man-thing — find a place to sit, before I change my mind.

Shaking, Iko clambered up the dragon's shoulder and swung a leg over his neck. He shuffled forwards to the point where he thought he would be able to hold on without injuring himself. He'd expected the dragon's scales would be smooth, like a fish's, but they had shallow parallel ridges, like some seashells. He hoped that would help him keep his grip.

Esald lumbered through a quarter-turn to face into the wind. *Hold tight. If you fall off, I might not notice in time to catch you.* He spread his wings, tilting them to test the current. Iko pressed himself closer to the dragon's skin. Esald ran, beating his wings in time with his footsteps. When he reached the edge of the open area, the ground fell away, and there was no sound but the wind.

Chapter 6

Iko shivered as the wind whipped his hair and clothing. He leaned forward, finding some shelter behind Esald's crest.

So, he said carefully, *what kind of service do you think might be enough to release you from your binding?*

We will talk of that later, Esald replied. *At present my attention is fully occupied by two things — staying in the air, and overcoming my urge to turn upside down and let you fall into the ocean, consequences be damned.*

They remained silent until the dragon's island came in sight. As they neared the ledge, Iko was now able to see through the illusory wall to the chamber within. Did that mean that the binding was becoming more complete?

Brace yourself, said Esald. *The sudden stop might throw you forward.* It could hardly be worse than the first landing here, but Iko hunkered down and held on tighter.

In the event, the dragon managed to slow himself enough outside the entrance that he hit the stone barely faster than walking pace, and easily came to a stop. He crouched, and Iko dismounted, sliding more than climbing. His joints were stiff, and muscles ached — a different set from the earlier flights. He hobbled in front of the dragon, whose lips had curled back from his teeth.

What do you mean, said Esald, *"what kind of service do I think might release me from my binding?"*

Iko frowned. *Exactly that. I would not attempt to snare you with a trick question.*

Do you not want me to destroy the pirates?

Iko took a step back. *I had hoped so, but when the other dragons talked of clearing an infestation of pigeons, or...*

They will pay for that insult. Double for doing it in front of a human. Esald opened his jaws, wide enough for Iko to fit in his mouth without bending, then snapped them shut with a crack that echoed from the walls. *Do you wish me to destroy the pirates?*

I, uh... really I just want them to leave us alone.

And how can you be sure they will do that if you allow them to live?

They're cowards, Iko said. *They only attack those weaker than themselves.*

And if you allow them to live, then once I have completed my service, you will again be weaker than they are.

But they won't know that, said Iko. *Nobody among humans has seen a dragon for a thousand years or more, but we still tell one another stories of your magnificence and terror. The mere sight of you, flying low over their harbour, might be enough to make them flee the entire archipelago.*

Esald snorted and waggled his head, as though trying to hold back a sneeze. *Very well. If you are certain that you do not wish me to harm them...*

Not unless they refuse to leave us alone, said Iko.

He lowered his head until his eyes were level with Iko's. *Then, bound as I am to you, I accept the obligation of this service. I will not rest until I have rid you of these pirates or death claims me.*

Iko went down on one knee and bowed his head. *I thank you, o great dragon. I will strive to be worthy of the honour you do me.*

Do not think to mock me, said Esald. His hot breath rolled over Iko, smelling of sand and ashes. *No rider ever bowed to a dragon, nor said he honoured him.*

Iko stood straight again. *But I am not a rider, o great dragon.*

I suppose not. If you were, I would have killed you the moment I laid eyes on you.

So they were back to that again. Iko reminded himself that the dragon was not his friend, nor even his ally. Esald served him because he had to, and would kill him in a heartbeat if he thought he would get away with it.

Now, said Esald, *to practical matters. How many are these pirates? What weapons and defences do they have?*

I... I don't know, exactly, said Iko. *I suppose there are a few hundred of them altogether. They use swords, axes and bows. They have at least three ships, one three-masted, the others two-masted. The ships have bigger bows that can shoot arrows, as well as jars of a substance that burns when the jar cracks open.*

Fire is no danger to me, said Esald. *And a human would have to be exceptionally lucky to harm me with a weapon it could carry. The arrows from the large bows might pierce my hide. Where is the pirates' nest — their stronghold, you would call it?*

I don't know. I'm not sure they even have one. No, they must have — their ships need repair and resupply.

Then you must have some notion of where it is.

Iko shook his head.

What does that gesture mean?

It means I don't know. Well — it can't be very far from the Lenis Islands, otherwise it wouldn't be worth their while to keep coming to us, and they always approach from the south-east, but apart from that, I don't know.

Then I cannot help you, said Esald.

What? said Iko. *Why not?*

I promised to stop the pirates from being a threat to you, not to find them for you.

Iko's mouth hung open for a moment. He snapped it shut before the dragon could ask what he meant by that. *Of all the small-minded, petty —* He took a deep breath to try to calm himself. *Why don't we just wait until they come to my village again?*

That might take a long time. Delay in fulfilling my obligation will cause me harm. Eventually, it will harm you too. Besides, repelling them from your village would not be as effective as attacking them in their nest, where they believe themselves to be safest and strongest.

Iko had to concede that last point. *Then how do we find them?*

"We" do not. You do.

How do I find them, then?

Of the two of us, you are the expert on humans.

Iko grimaced. *And once I've found them, then what?*

Go to a high place near their nest —

What? Iko interrupted. *I thought I'd just need to tell you where it is!*

Go to a high place near their nest, the dragon repeated, *and cast the spell you used when I first met you.*

If they catch me, they'll kill me.

You have many flaws, human, but I had not thought cowardice to be one of them. You were willing to stand before me when it seemed certain that your death would result.

If they kill me, said Iko, *I won't be able to summon you, and you won't be able to complete the service you agreed to perform.*

If you die, Esald replied, *the binding between us dissolves.*

Is that why you want me to go to the-the nest on my own?

I will not insult you by pretending that the possibility has not crossed my mind, said the dragon. *But the real reason is because a dragon cannot fly out of sight of land in your world.*

Why is that? Iko said. *You don't seem to have any problem doing it here.*

Nobody knows. Esald lifted a foot off the floor and extended the leg sideways, as though stretching. *I can cross from my world to yours at any point, so in principle, you could tell me where the pirates are, and I could travel to that point in my world and cross over.*

Why not do that, then?

It cannot have escaped your notice that there is very little land in our world, Esald said.

Trying not to rankle at the dragon's tone, Iko said, *It has not.*

Each piece of land that exists here corresponds to a piece of land that exists in your world, but not every piece of land in your world exists in ours. A wise dragon attempted to explain it to me once. To the best of my understanding, our world lies on top of yours, though not in a literal sense, and the worlds touch at certain points. No land exists in our world to the south-east of your home for at least several days' flight.

That was an interesting bit of information — could a dragon fly for several days at a time, or could they rest on the sea in their world? *So you'd have no way of knowing whether you were in the right place,* said Iko, *unless I go to the right place in my world and cast the summoning spell.*

It is not a summoning spell.

Iko rolled his eyes. *I wanted a dragon to appear. A dragon appeared when I cast it. What else would you suggest I call it?*

Esald ignored the question. *Unless you cast the spell from your side, I will not know where to cross over.*

If I do this, said Iko, *it will take at least a week for me to reach the pirates' stronghold. Will the binding allow you to be idle for that long?*

You will be working towards allowing me to fulfil my obligation. The binding does not punish me for not acting when it is not possible for me to act.

I see, said Iko, though he wasn't sure he did. *Then if there is nothing else you need to tell me, perhaps you should return me to my world.*

Chapter 7

Iko stood atop Ansrad Hill and watched Esald battle his way skywards, then vanish in a bright flash. He descended towards the village. Everything had a vivid green cast — probably his eyes had grown used to all the purple in the dragons' world, and this was just their reaction to its absence.

A few hundred yards from the village proper, he waved to a sun-browned middle-aged man working in a field by the road. The man blanched and nearly dropped his hoe.

"T-teacher Iko?"

Yes, it's me.

"Is it really you?"

I just said it was. Then he realised he was still speaking with his mind, in the manner of dragons. He got halfway through saying, "Yes, it's me," before he remembered it was a good idea to breathe in prior to using his voice, and the end of the sentence dissolved into coughing. The man approached, seemingly intent on slapping his back, but Iko waved him away.

"I heard the dragon had eaten you," the man said once the coughing had stopped.

"Obviously he didn't."

"No," the man replied, "no, I can see that." A moment passed, and Iko wondered whether to take his leave, and then the man said, "We thought he might've carried you to Nuhys."

Iko frowned. "Why?"

"Well, that's where dragons come from, isn't it? In the legends. But I said a dragon wouldn't come all that way just to eat one person, so maybe he came from somewhere nearer, and my sister said if he was going to eat you, he would've just done it there and then — it's not like dragons have table manners, is it? — so maybe he wanted you for something else."

Iko didn't think he could explain the concept of the dragons inhabiting a separate world to this fellow, so he said, "Is my mother all right, do you know?"

The man pursed his lips, as though wondering how much to reveal. "I haven't seen her, 'cos I've been out here. But from what I've heard, she's been very worried about you. Every day, she's been sitting at the edge of the village, looking up at the hill, waiting and watching for you to come back."

Iko's mouth hung open for a moment. "What do you mean, every day? I only left this morning."

"Maybe the dragon's done some magic on you." The man took a step back and gripped his hoe tighter. "You've been gone a week and a half."

"Impossible," said Iko. "I was on Ansrad Hill with the dragon this morning. Ask Serl — he was there with a dozen other men." He squinted at the sun to guess the time. "It's about four hours past noon now, agreed?"

The man nodded warily.

"I've been gone eight hours, then — nine at the most." He would've thought his flights with Esald added up to a lot more than that, but supposed now that they only seemed so long because there was nothing for him to do.

"I'm telling you, you've been gone ten days."

Iko gazed into the distance, unable to decide whether the man was mistaken or playing an unfunny joke. "Look, I didn't eat or drink or sleep while I was away. I don't feel tired, or hungry, or thirsty." He turned back to the man. "Actually, I read that if you don't drink anything for three days, you'll die. As you can see, I'm very much alive."

The man took another step away and, with his free hand, made what Iko took to be a superstitious sign. "Maybe you're a ghost."

Iko sighed. "If you believe such nonsense, I doubt anything I can say will convince you of your error. I hope you don't think I'm being rude — though I don't imagine ghosts have manners, any more than dragons do — but I need to go and find my mother." He left without waiting for a reply.

Just outside the village, Iko met a young woman with a basket under her arm. When she saw him, she dropped it and ran back along the main street. He hurried towards his house. A few more people recognised him and tried to ask what had happened, but he brushed them off with, "I'll explain later."

In the house, Mother was preparing dinner. She sat at the table, her back to him, and didn't turn at the sound of his entrance.

"Mother?" he ventured.

She paused in her peeling of a potato and tilted her head, as though unsure whether she'd heard something. Had the man in the field been right? Was he a ghost? He stepped in front of her.

Mother squealed and dropped what she'd been holding. She jumped to her feet and flung her arms around him, almost knocking him over. He guessed that meant he wasn't a ghost. "My baby, my beautiful baby," she said.

Iko embraced her. Where the side of her face rested against his chest, his tunic felt damp.

"I'm sorry," he mumbled.

She relaxed her grip and stared up at him. "Sorry? Is that all you can say? I've been sick with worry — I've barely slept or eaten since that monster carried you off. And what in the name of mercy were you thinking of, trying to *protect* it? Poldan tried to convince me you'd sacrificed yourself to save the rest of us, but Serl knows what he saw — you tried to stop them from attacking it." She seemed to have run out of breath and anger, and looked down, shaking her head and weeping quietly. Iko couldn't recall the last time she'd spoken so many words in one go.

Perhaps he had been protecting Esald. He'd also been trying to stop Serl from starting a fight he couldn't possibly win. But that wasn't what Mother needed to hear now. He rubbed her back and cleared his throat.

"I, uh... I think I may have lost track of time while I was away..."

She scowled at him, dashing tears from her eyes. "Is that your idea of an excuse? You're worse than your father." She pushed herself away from him and returned to preparing the potatoes.

Iko felt his face grow warm. "No, I mean, really, I lost track of time. As in, I'm not sure what day it is."

Mother gave him a disbelieving stare, then told him.

Iko staggered, as if he'd been punched in the stomach, and collapsed into the other chair. "Dagoreth," he muttered. "It's true."

"I'll not have that name spoken under this roof," Mother said, but her voice lacked the edge it had possessed when she'd previously chastised him or Father for blaspheming. She put down the potato and the knife. "Oh, Iko, what happened to you?" She rubbed her eyes with her cuff. "You used to be such a sweet little boy — no trouble at all."

And now he was more than making up for those years of sweetness and innocence. Mother might well prefer a son who came home drunk after brawling. He reached out to pat her shoulder, but then withdrew his hand.

Iko stood. "I need to talk to Serl. And the Proctor."

She turned to keep track of him as he reached for the door. "Promise me you won't ever leave me like that again. I was so worried for you — worse than any time when your father was late coming back from the sea." She paused, then glanced at the floor. "Poldan gave me rum to help me sleep. It didn't work."

For a moment, Iko considered lying to reassure her. Hand on the doorknob, he said, "I'm sorry. I can't promise I'll stay."

"Why not, for mercy's sake?"

"I don't think it's my decision any more."

Chapter 8

Iko sat in one of the monastery's meeting rooms with Sister Drubath and Serl, the village leader. Serl was clearly not comfortable with sitting down or being indoors. On the way here, he'd stared at everything as though he'd never seen it before — which, Iko realised, he probably hadn't.

Drubath glanced at the door and pointedly drummed her fingers on the table. She caught Iko's gaze and grinned nervously. She was being rude, but the Proctor was severely taxing their patience.

A door banged, and footsteps approached. The Proctor entered and sat down. Smoothing his robes, he glanced at the other people. "We're all here? Good."

"Do you normally keep visitors waiting this long?" said Serl.

"Pardon?" said the Proctor, studying him as though he was some new variety of beetle.

"We agreed to meet here at one o'clock. I was here a good bit before that, and so were your own people. I heard the bell in the tower ages ago."

The Proctor shifted in his chair. "I am sorry if you think that, but as Proctor of this monastery, I have many matters to attend to."

"You're telling me you've got something more important than deciding what to do about a dragon?"

The Proctor glowered at him. "I am telling you that I have many matters to attend to."

Drubath cleared her throat. "Perhaps we could discuss the dragon?"

"The dragon, yes." The Proctor turned to Iko. "So you intend to find the island where the pirates are hiding — whose location nobody has any idea of — and then summon this dragon that you claim is now in your service to..." His lip curled. "...frighten them into honest occupations."

Iko tried not to scowl at the implication that the dragon didn't exist. "I hope the dragon will overcome them without bloodshed. I am prepared to allow him to kill some of them, should it prove necessary."

"And what assurances can you offer that the dragon will stop at 'some?'" said the Proctor. "If the legends are to be believed, dragons hate all humans, not just those who break our laws. It knows where we live, and it knows we're weaker than the pirates."

"The dragon is bound to my will by magic," said Iko. "If I tell him not to kill anyone, he won't kill anyone."

"Are you sure it's bound?" said Serl. "Magic is slippery stuff. The beast could just be pretending."

In truth, Iko had no idea whether the binding was genuine. He'd thought something would feel different in his head or his heart, but it didn't. But this wasn't the time to show weakness or uncertainty. "He'll do as I say."

"Then in that case," said the Proctor, "how do we know that you won't use the dragon for your own ends, once you've disposed of the pirates?"

Iko's mouth hung open.

"Proctor," said Drubath, "if you knew anything about Teacher Iko, you'd know that such a thought would never occur to him."

"You're saying we should simply trust him to pick up the most powerful weapon known to mankind and use it exactly once."

"Trust is something of a foreign concept to you, isn't it, Proctor?" said Drubath.

The Proctor glared at her, the cords in his neck standing out. "Insubordination is not tolerated here."

"I didn't come here to listen to you lot bickering," said Serl. "There's no point fretting about next week's catch when you haven't brought today's into the harbour yet."

The Proctor sat back in his chair, evidently defeated — for

now, anyway.

"Well said," Drubath replied. "We have two questions to deal with — whether to use the dragon against the pirates, and if so, how to find their lair. The rest can wait."

Iko wiped his forehead. "I, uh, the dragon is already bound to defeat the pirates."

"So that answers the first question," said Serl. "What about the second? Do we wait for the pirates to come again and follow them home?"

"They would kill you if they saw you," said the Proctor. "That's why no one has ever been stupid enough to try it."

"The dragon said we can't sit around waiting," said Iko. "If there's something we can do — I can do — to move towards the goal, I have to do it."

"Makes me wonder just who's bound to who," Serl muttered.

"So," said the Proctor, "if you cannot follow the pirates to their lair, how do you propose to find them? Ask our neighbours? Sail the seas blindly until you sink or run out of food?"

"Asking our neighbours might not be such a bad idea," said Drubath. "If we ask them which direction the pirates approached from when they came from the sea, we can triangulate their origin."

Once she'd explained the concept to Serl, he said, "But ships don't travel in straight lines — not for more than a few hours, anyway. Winds and currents and tides push them around."

"But it'd give us a starting point," she said.

He nodded. "I'll send word to the other settlements that have been raided."

"You probably shouldn't tell them about the dragon just yet," said Iko.

"I wasn't going to."

"Well," said the Proctor, standing, "that seems to be everything we need to discuss. Report back to me once you have some news." He left the room without waiting for an answer.

For several moments, Serl stared at the doorway the

Proctor had passed through. "Kashalbe forgive me," he said, "but if it was me who'd bound this dragon, I'd be sore tempted to set it on him instead of the pirates."

Two weeks later, Iko, Drubath and Serl sat in the same meeting room, a large chart of the local seas on the table. Serl had weighted the chart's corners down and was busy pinning lengths of string across it to represent the directions that the neighbouring villages had said the pirates came from. The Proctor had said he would attend the meeting, but after a quarter of an hour there was no sign of him, so the others had started without him.

As Serl worked, Drubath shot Iko a concerned look. "Are you feeling all right, Teacher? You look as though you haven't slept for days."

Iko ran a hand through his hair. It was nearer a week since he'd last slept well. His joints were stiff, and his head ached most of the time. He often found himself gasping for breath, and his thighs ached like they did after he'd ridden on Esald's neck. Fretting over Mother's worry for him hadn't helped. His dreams had been filled with visions of flying through purple skies, battling other dragons, sometimes sending them spiralling into the sea, sometimes being smashed out of the air himself.

Disturbing as those images were, they were mild in comparison to the scenes of battle that took place in the human world. The dragons fought one another much more viciously, and attacked the enemies of their human masters indiscriminately, military and civilian alike. Smoke from burning settlements was usually visible even beyond the horizon.

"I'm fine," Iko said.

From the way Drubath rolled her eyes, she plainly didn't believe him, but she said nothing, returning her attention to Serl.

Iko wondered why he'd been seeing battles from the human world, when Esald had said he was too young to have fought for the dragonriders or in the Liberation. Perhaps the visions were Esald's dreams or imaginings of what life had been like for the dragons under the riders.

Serl finished laying strings and jabbed a confident finger at the spot on the map where the majority of them intersected. When he lifted his hand, he revealed a little cluster of islands, about twelve degrees east and seven degrees south of their position. "Close enough to be worth the journey, but not so close that any of us would think it was the obvious place."

"They're quite near Perakhandra," said Drubath. "Why don't they raid there instead?"

"Maybe they do," said Serl. "Maybe they take turns between Perakhandra and us."

"Or maybe Perakhandra has better defences," said Iko.

"Like a dragon of their own, eh?" said Serl.

Iko didn't answer, but Serl's words prompted a troubling thought. If he had found out how to summon a dragon, someone else could rediscover the same secret... and that person's motives might not be as selfless as his. The knowledge was all there in the monastery's archives, and who among the teachers and the monks would dare suggest destroying it?

"Well, you'd better get ready," Serl said to him. "We leave on the morning tide."

"We?" said Iko.

"You didn't think you were going on your own, did you? We'll take my father's old lugger. People keep telling me it's too big for these waters, but I knew it'd come in useful for something one day."

"You're coming with me?" said Iko.

"What's wrong — you think I don't wash?" said Serl. "I'm the best sailor in the village."

"And the most modest," said Drubath.

"Aren't you supposed to be, well, leading the village?" said Iko.

"My dad always told me that 'leading' means 'being at the front,'" Serl replied. "If the village has to fight, the leader goes in first."

"We won't be doing any fighting," said Iko.

"And what do you think will happen when your dragon shows up?" said Serl.

Chapter 9

Iko halted, gasping, and leaned over, hands on his knees. Further up the rocky trail, Serl glanced over his shoulder.

"Come on," said Serl. "We haven't got all day."

"Are you sure — this is — the right island?"

Serl turned and came a few paces towards Iko. "We saw the ship at anchor. We agreed it was one of theirs."

In truth, as Iko could scarcely tell a Nuhysean dinghy from a Perakhandran frigate, he hadn't felt qualified to disagree. "But it was just — sitting there next to — the cliffs. There's no docks — no other boats in sight. What's it doing in the — middle of nowhere?"

"The middle of nowhere would be a good place for pirates to set up a base, don't you think?" said Serl, starting back up the trail. "And there are plenty of reasons — I mean honest reasons — for a ship to be at anchor away from a dock."

Iko had enough of his breath back to resume the climb. His legs and feet were still sore. He wanted to sit, but he knew from having tried it that the stones were even hotter than the air above them. He told himself it wasn't as bad as being carried by Esald, and not nearly as bad as taking off or landing with the dragon, but that did nothing to ease the aches.

"Did we have to take such a steep route to the top?" Iko said.

"If you want to climb the other side and let all the pirates know we're here, go ahead." Serl had described the island as a "lopsided lump of sandstone" when they first saw it — mostly low-lying, but with a jumble of rocks at one side that was somewhere between a hill and a mountain. It was this hill-or-mountain that they were struggling up now, hoping to be able to see the pirates' harbour from the top.

They passed a patch of bare earth, perhaps twenty feet across, that nestled in a hollow among the rocks. "Strange," Iko muttered.

"What?" said Serl.

"We saw no vegetation from the ship."

"Boat," Serl sighed, obviously tired of correcting him. "Which makes this a good place for pirates to hide, because no one else is going to come nosing, thinking it might be a nice place to live."

"Yes, but that wasn't what I was talking about." Iko pointed to the patch of earth. "Something could grow there. So why doesn't it?"

Serl shrugged. "Poor soil? It can't be very deep. And the seeds have to come from somewhere — carried by animals or birds, or borne on the wind, or planted by people. None of those seem very likely out here."

"No," said Iko. "No, I suppose you're right."

"Anyway, come on. We're wasting time."

Eventually, they reached a ridge. Serl dropped to the ground and motioned Iko to do the same. He crawled to the top of the ridge and peeked over, then shoved himself back down.

"'Are you sure this is the right island?'" Serl said, sarcastically repeating Iko's earlier words. "See for yourself — but be careful."

Iko crept to the spot that Serl had used. A breeze removed just enough heat to make the ground bearable to lie on. Gravel and dust shifted under his legs and stomach, and he gripped the top of the ridge and pulled himself up. Slowly he peered over it.

On the other side, the ground fell away precipitously. Far below lay a near-circular lake, a couple of miles across. The still, clear water let Iko see the bottom for a good way from the shore. On the other side, a narrow high-walled channel led out to sea. It made quite a sharp angle with the shore, meaning that the lake would be difficult to spot from outside. That made the lake an ideal hiding place for the nine ships anchored on the near side, moored to a series of short, rickety wharves.

A flicker of movement in the channel caught Iko's eye. The ship they'd seen at anchor earlier was on its way into the lake, and he guessed it had been waiting for the tide to fill the channel to a sufficient depth.

"So are those the pirate ships?" Iko said, allowing himself to slide level with Serl.

"What else would they be?" said Serl. "There's nobody here for them to trade with. It doesn't look as though they've even got any way to supply or repair their ships. They've got no reason to be here, except hiding from everyone else."

"I suppose you're right. One thing puzzles me, though — there's no seaweed at the bottom of the lake."

Serl sighed. "Never mind that. Just — wave your hands and say the words and then we can go home."

Behind them, a man said, "Ye won't be going home for a long time."

Panicked, Iko lost his grip and slid a few feet down the slope.

"Don't move," said the man. "Not unless ye want a spear in yer kidneys." His voice was deep and rough, with an accent Iko didn't recognise.

"We're not moving," Serl said, straining his neck to look over his shoulder.

"Turn around so I can get a look at ye. Slowly."

Serl and Iko obeyed. Iko's hands shook as he propped himself up to turn over, expecting to be stabbed at any moment. Before them stood four swarthy men — no, three men and one woman — dressed in ragged clothing and carrying an assortment of weapons. The man at the front, older than the rest, had a spear, taller than himself, with a long serrated blade.

"Who are ye and what are ye doing here?" said the spear-carrier.

"W-we're from the monastery on-" Iko began. He stopped as Serl elbowed him.

"Are you pirates?" Serl said.

The man with the spear laughed. His comrades joined in uneasily. Iko guessed he was the group's leader. "That depends who ye ask." He jabbed the spear in Serl's direction. "Since ye don't seem to want to say who ye are, how about we move on to what yer doing here?"

"We've come to stop your piracy," said Serl.

The leader gawked at them. "What — just the two of ye?" He laughed again. "Maybe I'll let ye live — the chief needs a new jester."

"We're not joking," said Serl. "We've got a dragon."

Just for a moment, the man seemed afraid. Then he leaned slightly forward and to one side, as though trying to see past Iko and Serl. He stood up straighter and shook his head. "Where is it, then?"

"He," said Iko.

"What?"

"He. The dragon is a male."

"Of course," said the leader. "Careless of me not to notice. So where's *he,* then? In yer pocket, maybe? Or are ye just pleased to see us?" One of the other men sniggered.

Iko took a couple of deep breaths to calm himself and uttered the summoning spell.

The leader frowned at him. "What was that? I don't speak Asdanundish."

"It's not Asdanundish. It's the spell that calls the dragon."

The leader nodded slowly. "Of course it is," he said, as though humouring a child in a game of make-believe.

Iko felt his fist involuntarily clench. The first time he'd spoken the spell, Esald had appeared within a few heartbeats. "Perhaps you should step away," he told the leader. "I wouldn't want the dragon to crush you when he lands."

"We certainly wouldn't want that, would we lads?" the leader said to his comrades. One of them began walking, but the leader grabbed his upper arm before he'd gone more than two paces. He was clearly having trouble deciding whether Iko and Serl were just stalling for time, or genuinely mad.

Where was Esald? Iko risked a glance skyward, seeing nothing. "The dragon makes quite a strong wind when he lands." His throat had gone dry, and he swallowed to moisten it. "You should go maybe a hundred yards that way, so he doesn't knock you over." He pointed downhill.

"Perhaps ye'd better come with us, then," the leader said. He nodded to his comrades, who moved behind Iko and Serl and began tying their hands. "After all, there's a long drop behind ye, and I wouldn't want the wind to push ye over it." He started downhill. "Ye might damage the ships."

Maybe he'd got the spell wrong, Iko thought as he half-walked, half-skidded down the slope. He tried to calm himself — difficult when he couldn't use his arms for balance — and spoke the spell again.

The words had scarcely left his lips when he felt a cold hard line against his throat. Without thinking, he jerked backwards and banged his shoulder against something.

"Don't move!" Serl shouted.

Iko risked a glance downwards and saw a heavy knife being held under his chin. He tried not to tremble. Would Esald still come if he was dead?

"Ye should listen to him," the leader growled next to Iko's ear. "Let me make a few things clear. I don't believe in dragons, and I don't believe in magic. What I do believe in is my captain, and how upset he'll be if he finds out I captured a couple of spies, but had to kill them because they were trying to escape."

"W-we're not s-spies," Iko said.

"Shut it." The man slapped the underside of Iko's chin with the flat of the blade, rattling his teeth. "Which means that if any more of that gibberish comes out of yer mouth — or any words at all, for that matter — I'm going to assume yer shouting orders to yer friend about running away. I'm also going to assume both of ye know everything there is to know about yer mission. Which means I only need one of ye alive." He withdrew the knife, and Iko heard him sheath it. "Now move."

Chapter 10

A distant candle gave just enough light for Iko to see Serl next to him. They sat in a small room, hollowed out of the rock under the hill. The door didn't fit the entrance, and Serl had thought they might be able to lift it out — except that the guard in the corridor would have had something to say about that.

"Well?" said Serl. "What now?"

Iko sighed. "I don't know." He'd thought that if the pirates caught them before Esald arrived, they would simply kill them. But apart from the leader of the group that had captured them, nobody seemed interested in them. It was as if they were an inconvenience more than anything else.

"Why didn't your spell work?"

"Again, I don't know. I thought I got the words right —"

Serl interrupted with, "You *thought*?"

The guard banged on the door. "Quiet in there!"

Iko waited a few moments before whispering, "Yes, well, I didn't want to write it down in case I lost it, so I committed it to memory. It worked the first time I used it, on Ansrad Hill."

"Oh, Kashalbe's arse," Serl groaned.

Iko frowned at the vulgarity. "It's only twenty-one syllables — not even two lines of one of your drinking songs."

"Yeah, well, if you get those wrong, nobody waves a spear in your face and shoves you into a dark hole."

"I said quiet!" the guard yelled.

Iko leaned against the wall and tried to think of another reason why the spell hadn't worked. Could he be sure he'd got the words right? Maybe Esald couldn't find him. Or maybe Esald had been lying when he'd promised to come.

Shouting came from far away. At first Iko thought the chief was giving orders, but this was several men, their cries overlapping. Then there were three deep blasts on a horn. A pause, then three more blasts. A dull thud reverberated through the rock, and Iko felt a handful of grit fall on his arm.

The guard banged the door again. "Stay here."

"What's happening?" Serl said.

"Three notes means we're under attack," the guard replied. Iko heard him take a couple of paces away, then he added, "Whoever it is probably won't want to rescue ye, so don't go skiving." He ran off.

"How very convenient," said Serl.

"Do you want to see if we really can lift the door out?" said Iko.

"What do you think?"

The door was heavy, but the three-inch gap at the top gave them plenty of room to raise it from its hinges. They left it propped against a wall and walked slowly in the direction the guard had gone.

"He shouldn't have left his post, should he?" said Iko. "Not without an order from a superior."

"They don't seem the most disciplined lot," Serl replied. "And maybe they're not used to having prisoners. They've never taken anyone from the village for ransom."

"Maybe they thought we couldn't afford to pay."

They crept through the tunnels and caverns. The pirates were grudging with candles, often putting them only at junctions to make them do duty for more than one direction. It made sense, Iko supposed, with nothing local to the island that they could turn into oil or tallow.

They came to a larger-than-average cave with bedding and clothes scattered around. Iko saw few personal possessions, and he wondered what had happened to all the things the pirates had stolen from the village. Serl spotted a short sword and a knife lying on a blanket. He took the sword and passed the knife to Iko.

"I don't know how to use this," Iko said.

"The pointy end goes in the other fellow."

"Very funny. I mean, I've never been in a fight."

"What, never?"

"Not since I was a boy. And never against someone trying to kill me."

Serl sighed. "Stay behind me, then. It looks as though most of them have run off to deal with the attack. If they retreat, we'll run into them coming against us."

Iko realised it had been a while since he'd heard any sounds of the attack, or of the pirates responding to it. Was it over? Why hadn't they seen anyone returning?

Serl pointed to a torch in a bracket on the wall, and Iko took it. They moved into a series of tunnels with no light of their own.

"Do you know where you're going?" Iko asked.

"Not really," Serl replied, "but there's a breeze on my face, so this must lead to the outside."

There were no signs of habitation in this area. The tunnels grew narrower and lower, to the point where Iko and Serl had to bend over. They came to a point where the roof had caved in, and found just enough room to squeeze over the pile of rubble.

Serl put a finger to his lips, then pointed to a shard of daylight that lay across the floor. The roof lowered again, so that they had to go on their hands and knees for a few yards. They emerged into a cave, too large for the torch to reveal its full size. At the opposite side was a near-vertical slot, about man-sized, leading to the outside. Serl peered around the edges of this, then ducked back inside.

"We're still by that lake we saw from the hill," he whispered. "I couldn't see any of the ships, so we might be far enough around the shore that they won't see us."

Iko wasn't so sure of that, but he stubbed the torch out on the ground. Serl went through the slot — it was narrow enough that he had to go sideways — and motioned Iko to follow.

Iko squeezed through the slot, with a good deal more effort than Serl. Evidently, working a boat and nets kept a man thinner than drumming knowledge into a class of children.

As soon as sunlight touched his face, an inhuman, terror-stricken scream filled his head.

Chapter 11

"Iko!" Serl shook his shoulder, then grabbed his forearm and tried to pull him free of the slot. "What's wrong?"

Iko screwed his eyes shut and put his other hand over his ear. That made no difference to the screaming. Gradually the noise resolved itself into words, each one like a hammer striking his skull.

Man-thing! Where in all the freezing hells are you, worthless worm? Help me!

"It's Esald!" Iko shouted, opening his eyes.

"Ssh!" Serl glanced around, then resumed trying to pull Iko out.

"Ow!"

"Where is he?"

"I don't know." Iko sucked in his stomach and wriggled loose. "He needs our help — I think he's hurt."

"Oh, Kashalbe's arse," Serl muttered. "Where is he?"

"I'll try to find out." Iko closed his eyes and thought, *Esald, can you hear me? Where are you?*

No answer came, just more screaming. "He must be where the pirates are," Iko said. "That must be what the attack was about." Now he noticed thick smoke rising from beyond a spur of rock, where he guessed the ships were. He took a deep breath and set off at a run along the shingle-strewn beach.

"Come back!" Serl called after him.

Iko ignored him. He'd gone maybe a dozen yards when pain stabbed into his left upper arm. He cried out and stumbled. He clapped his right hand over the spot, managing to stagger a few paces before he tripped and fell.

"What in the Goddess' name are you playing at?" Serl said,

61

approaching. He held out a hand, and Iko allowed him to pull him to his feet.

Rolling up his sleeve, Iko saw a reddish-purple mark about the size of his fingertip, as if he'd been struck by a stone from a slingshot. The pain faded, becoming more of an ache. Now that he could think about the matter more clearly, the pain seemed to go right through his arm. Sure enough, there was another small mark on the opposite side.

"I think, being bound to Esald, I'm feeling the wounds that he received."

"We should leave," said Serl. "While we still can."

Before Iko could refuse, pain flared across his cheek, as though he'd been punched. Instinctively, he jerked backwards. Serl grabbed his shoulder just in time to stop him from falling.

Iko shook his head. "If Esald dies, it'll hurt me."

"How much?"

Iko gawked at him. "That's not really the point."

"No, the point is if the pirates catch us, they'll kill us — and a lot more slowly than the dragon would."

"I can't abandon him." Iko ran towards the point where the spur met the water, stumbling and slipping over the loose stones.

"Get down from there!" Serl demanded as Iko climbed the spur and peered over the top.

The docks were about a hundred yards further along the shore. One — no, two of the ships they'd seen from the hill were on fire. A couple of hundred men stood on the shore, seemingly at a loss as to what to do. Why weren't they trying to extinguish the fires? And where was Esald? Iko called to him with his mind.

Snivelling coward! You laid a trap for me! The dragon's voice, though still loud, sounded weaker than when Iko had last heard it.

No I didn't. Are you hurt?

Of course I am hurt, faithless human! Was that not your plan?

It wasn't, said Iko. *I — I swear it by Kashalbe's crown. Why would you think I betrayed you?*

Iko felt a hand grab his ankle and stifled a yell. He looked down to see Serl tugging him. He kicked free of the man's grip. "I've got to stay here, otherwise I don't think Esald can hear me."

Muttering obscenities, Serl crawled up the spur to lie next to Iko. "Where is he, then?"

"That's what I'm trying to find out," Iko said. *Esald? Why do you think I betrayed you?*

This... this land is cursed.

Cursed? How?

A shadow flickered among the smoke, and pain wrenched Iko's upper arm.

"There." Serl pointed to where the shadow had been. "Goddess, he's lying on one of the ships!"

"Is it one of the ones that are on fire?" Iko said, even as he recalled that fire posed no threat to a dragon.

"I don't think so. That's why the pirates are all hanging around on the shore."

Many years ago, Esald said, *humans fought a war that spanned most of your world.*

The Elangic Civil War? Iko said. He'd always thought it odd that the largest war in history had technically been confined to one country.

The name is unimportant. Magical weapons were used that could shatter a city from a thousand miles away. One of them struck this island. As well as destroying the physical environment, it corrupted the world's magical energies around its point of impact. My ability to fly in your world depends partly on magic.

This lake must be the crater the weapon made, Iko said. *So when you crossed over to our world, you fell out of the sky.*

Yes, Esald replied after a moment.

And impaled one of your front legs on a ship's mast.

How do you know that?

We're bonded, remember? said Iko. *So you've destroyed three of their ships — the one you landed on and two more you set on fire — and because you can't move, the pirates have retreated beyond the range of your claws and breath, and... they're waiting for you to die.*

They will be waiting a long time, Esald said. *But I believe you are correct.*

"What are you *doing?*" Serl said.

"I'm talking to Esald," Iko replied.

"You look as though you're constipated."

Scowling, Iko slid out of the pirates' sight and explained the situation as quickly as he could.

"That weapon thingummy must be why nothing grows here," Serl said. "Anyway, let's go."

"We can't," Iko said.

"Why not? The dragon's destroyed three ships and killed dozens of pirates. He might well take out a few more along the way. And before too long, he'll die himself, so we don't have to worry about him coming after us once he's fulfilled his side of the bargain."

Iko clenched a fist. "And if Esald dies, there won't be anything to stop the surviving pirates coming back to our homes to take revenge. If he lives, we have the threat of-of summoning him again if they don't leave us alone."

Serl sighed and nodded. "So how do we save him, then?"

"We need to get a better look at the situation and see how badly injured he is."

"Difficult. We could go back through the caves, but we'd probably get lost on the way, or run into pirates. Trying to get up the hill for a look would take too long. We could go round the other side of the lake, but I don't think we'd be able to cross the entrance channel."

"Only one thing for it, then," said Iko.

"What?"

Iko stood and clambered to the top of the spur.

"Get down, you idiot!"

Iko waved his arms. "Over here! We want to talk!"

Chapter 12

The guards manhandled Iko and Serl into the presence of the pirates' chief, a stocky, bare-chested man with a thick beard and a collection of eye-watering tattoos. He stood on the end of one of the wharves, staring at the ships that Esald had wrecked. He turned to examine the two men, looking as though he couldn't believe his underlings had brought them to him instead of killing them on sight.

"So," he said, "yer the weevils who brought this monster here, wrecked three of my ships, and killed a hundred of my men." His voice sounded as though he'd swallowed a bucket of gravel. "Tell me why I shouldn't make footstools out of yer bones."

Iko licked his lips. If he survived this day, he'd never be afraid of the Proctor again. "I control th-the dragon, Sir. I can remove him without your losing any m-more men or ships."

The chief folded his arms. "The beast's wounded. Hasn't moved in an hour. Seems all I have to do is wait and the problem goes away by itself."

"Do you know how long a dragon takes t-to die, Sir?" Iko asked.

"Is it longer than twelve hours? 'Cos if it is, the ship he's lying on will have sunk anyway by then."

"The water isn't deep enough to drown him," Serl said.

"You might have to consider how much food you've got," Iko said. He tried not to feel pleased at lying by omission. He hadn't said the food would run out before Esald died, just that the pirates should consider how much of it they had.

The chief grinned. "Months in the caves."

Iko gulped. "Dragons, ah, sometimes just pretend to be

dead."

"If that was true, ye'd have said it sooner." He grinned again. "Suppose I'd better give ye a chance to prove ye can control the beast. I shouldn't have to say this, but try making it do anything dangerous and ye'll both be dead before ye've finished giving the order." The guards shoved Iko and Serl in the direction of the shore, and the chief walked alongside them.

Esald? Iko said with his mind. *Can you hear me?*

I hear you. The dragon's voice sounded weaker than when he had last spoken.

I'm going to try to free you. I need to convince the pirates that you're under my control. How much can you move?

Not much. Being impaled on a tree tends to restrict one's freedom.

That wasn't what I meant. Can you swish your tail and hit something, or breathe fire?

I doubt I have the strength to move any limbs. I have never been able to breathe fire.

Iko stumbled, and a guard punched his shoulder. He resisted the urge to complain. *What? I thought all dragons could do that.*

You thought wrongly, said Esald.

How did the ships catch fire, then?

I do not know.

They reached the shore, where a loose group of a hundred or so pirates loitered. A few pirates shouted insults at Iko and Serl. As they turned to walk towards Esald, something whizzed past Iko, a few inches from his face, and struck the wharf with a splat.

The chief held up a hand, and the group halted. "If the man who threw that steps forward now, he'll be the only one punished."

From the corner of his eye, Iko saw some of the pirates pushing another towards the front of the group. *So anyway,* he said to Esald, *what can you do?*

The pirate who'd thrown the object shrugged free of the others and stood before the chief, head held high. The chief looked him up and down before saying, "Number three." He motioned Iko and Serl to continue. As they did so, Iko heard fists connecting with flesh, accompanied by grunts, as if the victim was determined not to give his assailants the satisfaction of hearing him cry out.

I could... Esald said. *I could perhaps produce a loud roar. I am told that some... it induces terror in some humans.*

Esald sounded sleepy. *Stay with me,* Iko said. He tried to pick up his pace, but someone laid a heavy hand on his shoulder.

"What's yer hurry?" the chief said.

I am not going anywhere, Esald said. *That is my... my entire problem.*

A loud roar will be fine, Iko said.

Now?

No — I'll tell you when.

I might need some notes. Some notice.

They passed the first of the burning ships. It listed, and some of its rigging hung over its wharf, which Iko thought might allow the fire to spread. Nobody seemed to be paying attention to it.

How much notice? Iko asked.

A verse, maybe.

A moment passed before Iko realised that Esald had to be referring to the song the dragons used to time ascents and descents. How long was a verse? He had no idea. They came to another burning ship. This one was mostly underwater, its deck awash, its masts and rigging all but gone.

The next ship was the one Esald had landed on. It sat low in the water, its masts at awkward angles. At first, Iko couldn't see Esald, as he'd brought the sails down, and they covered his torso and wings like a shroud. The dragon's head and one of his front legs lolled over the side of the ship. A dark stain had spread over a large area of the sails and slicked over the planks. It was obvious why the chief was happy to wait for Esald to die rather than let Iko do anything about him.

You'd better roar, Iko said.

The chief clapped a hand on Iko's shoulder again. "This is near enough."

Iko licked his lips and took a deep breath. "Since you forbade me from telling the dragon to do anything dangerous, I will order him to roar."

"I'll be impressed if he can even belch now."

Waving his arms in what he hoped looked like magical gestures, Iko shouted, "O great dragon, I command you to roar, loud enough to cleanse all here present of their disbelief!"

Nothing happened.

Behind Iko, someone sniggered.

"Obey me, dragon, or face the consequences!" In the dragons' speech, he added, *Now would be good.*

Still nothing happened.

The chief sighed. "Kill them."

Serl grabbed Iko's forearm and tried to run. A couple of the guards stepped in front of them. Behind them, metal hissed on leather as a sword came from its sheath. Iko glimpsed movement on the ship. Then he felt, more than heard, a rumbling that shook the cliffs. The sword clattered to the ground as the guards fell to their knees, hands over their ears.

Iko turned to face the pirates. Their faces looked as if they'd found maggots in their meals. They moved slowly and deliberately, as though afraid of aggravating injuries. One had bent to retrieve the sword, and as he straightened, Iko noticed a dark patch on the inside of his trouser leg. He tried not to smile.

Thank you, o great dragon, Iko thought. Esald didn't reply.

"I'll let ye live," the chief said, working his jaw as though unsure whether all his teeth were still present. "For now, anyway. So what's yer plan for getting rid of the beast?"

"First, there are some conditions for our help," Iko said.

The chief grimaced. "Aren't there always?"

"Just one condition, really." Iko took a deep breath. "I want you to give up piracy and raiding."

The chief stared at him, then burst out laughing. "That's a good one," he said when he'd calmed down. "Now what do ye really want?"

Iko scowled. "I'm serious."

"Then ye might as well tell the beast to kill us all. Too many of us have prices on our heads to have a hope of earning an honest living."

"Very well. In that case, I want you to stop raiding the Lenis Islands."

"That's where yer from, is it?"

Iko nodded. "The dragon will be protecting them."

"Seems to me I could just kill both of ye now, wait for the dragon to die, then carry on raiding the islands anyway."

Trying not to clench his fists, Iko replied, "If you kill me, the dragon wouldn't be under my control any more. There's no telling what he'd do."

The chief looked past Iko to the ship and rolled his eyes. "Seems all he wants to do right now is bleed to death. But I admire yer guts. So if ye can get the beast out of here by... let's be generous and say the start of the next ebb tide, I'll leave yer islands alone."

"How much time is that?" Iko said.

"About six hours."

That wasn't as much as Iko thought he needed, but was more than he'd thought he'd get. "Very well. I'll need half-a-dozen brave, strong men, with a couple of axes or a two-man saw."

The chief spoke to the man who'd dropped and picked up the sword. "Go fetch those from the *Lucky Lad*." As the man waddled towards the other ships, the chief called after him, "And clean yerself up before you come back here!"

While they waited, Iko spoke to Esald. *I'll be coming aboard the ship soon to free you. There'll be some other men with me. Don't harm them.*

Even if I wanted to, Esald replied, *I do not believe myself to be in a state where that is possible.*

Six men approached and stood before Iko.

"These do ye?" the chief asked.

Their bravery remained to be seen, but judging from their muscles, there was no doubting their strength. One of them rested a hand atop a saw that was longer than he was tall. Iko nodded his approval. He drew himself up to his full height.

"You will accompany us onto that ship behind me and cut

my dragon free from the wreckage. He is under my control, but he is a very dangerous creature who could easily kill you. If you do exactly as I say, you will come to no harm." He prayed Esald had been telling the truth about that. "Do you understand?"

Variously, the men indicated that they did.

Iko turned to face Esald. He waved his arms and shouted, "Hear me, O great dragon! I bring humans into your presence! They are under my protection! Great shall be my wrath should any harm come to them!" Iko glanced over his shoulder and beckoned, then strode towards the ship.

Once they were on the wharf, the first problem was how to get aboard. The ship had been jerked away from the dock when Esald fell on it, snapping most of its mooring ropes and pulling the gangplank off the wharf.

"We need to reattach the mooring," said one of the pirates. He looked to be the oldest, and Iko guessed he was the group's leader.

"The ship's not going anywhere," said Serl. It lay low — the portholes near the stern were only a foot above the waterline.

"She's not stable," said the pirate. "She's taking on water, and that monster makes her top-heavy. If we just run out the gangplank again, it could easily collapse or slip when someone steps on it. I don't fancy swimming in this water at the best of times, and I don't expect ye do either."

"Very well," said Iko. "Do what's necessary to make the ship secure."

The pirate nodded to one of the others, who took a running jump onto the rear part of the deck, just in front of the poop deck. He found a rope and tied it to a bollard, then threw the other end to one of his comrades, who tied it to the wharf. He climbed up to the poop deck and attached another rope to the wharf. He started towards the bow of the ship, then stopped and turned to Iko.

"I need to climb over the monster to get to the gangplank. Is it safe?"

Esald? Iko thought. *A man's going to climb over you. Don't be alarmed.* There was no reply.

"He is a dragon, not a monster," Iko said to the man. "But

yes, go ahead."

The man went out of sight behind the sails that covered Esald's enormous bulk, then reappeared near the forecastle. He pulled the gangplank up over the side of the ship, then ran it out to the wharf. Another pirate tied it to a bollard and gestured for everyone to board.

Iko went first, reasoning that he'd better appear to be in charge. He had never been on a ship this big, and was surprised at how little it rocked with the waves. The deck sloped towards the wharf, doubtless from Esald's weight. Pieces of wood and rope were scattered across the deck, probably from the masts.

Iko turned to look at Esald. The dragon's body was about as long as the ship was wide, and his back legs and tail hung over the starboard side. Tangled rigging and bloodstained sails covered most of his body. The weight of his impact had staved in many of the planks under him. His right wing, twisted at an unnatural angle, covered about a third of the fore part of the deck. A long stump of the mainmast poked up from the middle of the sails.

"The first thing we need to do," said Iko, "is lift the sails off the dragon, so I can see how bad his injuries are."

At first the pirates wanted to pull the sails off Esald, but Iko persuaded them to stand three on either side of the dragon, lift them off, then throw them onto the wharf.

As Iko had suspected, the stump of the mainmast had impaled Esald's left front leg, near the shoulder. It was about a foot thick, and protruded maybe ten feet above his leg. If dragons had a similar anatomy to other four-legged creatures — which he knew was not a wise assumption — the mast had missed the bone, but might well have severed a major blood vessel.

"Now we need to get the mast out of his leg," said Iko.

"Best way to do that is to saw the top off," said the group's leader, "then either lift his leg off it, or saw it at the bottom and pull it out."

Iko nodded. "Do it." *Esald? A couple of men are going to climb on top of you to start taking the mast out of you.* No answer came.

The leader told the man who carried the saw and another to start sawing. At first, they didn't move, and then the one with the saw said, "Is it safe?"

"Ye saw what the blasted thing did to *Karkher's Whip* and *Barracuda,*" the leader snapped. "Of course it's not safe."

Iko waved his arms. "O great dragon, I command you to do no harm to these men while they aid you." To the pirates, he said, "I already ordered him not to hurt you while you were on the ship, but that gives them another, ah, layer of armour."

The men climbed on top of Esald, and sat on his leg, one on either side of the mast. Iko felt a curious numbness in his upper arm around the point of his sympathetic injury. After a couple of false starts, the men began sawing, about a foot above where the mast emerged from Esald's flesh. A minute or two later, they stopped.

"It moved," one of them said.

"Barely," the leader replied. "Ye've had rougher crossings of the Bay of Enthrad."

"We don't try to do major repairs when we're underway," the man replied.

"And we don't usually have to repair things that would just as soon eat us," his partner added.

"Get on with it," the leader said. "Sooner ye stop mithering, sooner ye can get back to yer tankards."

The men resumed sawing. Iko's upper arm grew warm, but when he touched it, it felt no different from the surrounding flesh. The men stopped a couple more times, convinced Esald was moving. Iko saw no evidence of this, and the leader persuaded them to go on. Eventually, they had cut through enough of the mast for the other men to topple it onto the deck, where it landed with a loud crack. Iko felt momentarily light-headed. The pain in his upper arm sharpened, then faded.

"Now comes the hard part," said the leader. The four men who hadn't been sawing worked their arms under Esald's leg and tried to lift it. They managed about six inches before giving up.

The sawyers passed the saw under the leg and started

cutting the mast. Halfway through, Esald's leg slipped down the mast, stopping when it hit the saw. Iko's arm felt as though he'd been stabbed. A noise like a thousand swords striking a thousand shields filled his head. Strong arms grabbed him.

"Are you all right?" said Serl.

Iko shook his head to try to clear the noise, which just made the problem worse. He held up a hand to indicate Serl should wait, and gradually the noise subsided.

"We need to prop up his leg, yes?" said Serl.

"Yes," said Iko. Even that simple word took a lot of effort.

"You heard him," Serl said to the pirates. "See if you can move that piece of the mast under it."

All six men gathered around the section of the mast, but couldn't even raise it off the deck. A couple of them tried pushing it, without success.

"Maybe we can use what's left of the rigging to lift the leg," said the leader. "Maybe even pull it off the mast altogether."

"Or just as likely pull the foremast down on top of us," said one of the sawyers.

"Reckon it'll hold long enough for what we have to do," the leader said.

As the men set to work, Serl muttered, "And why didn't we think of that sooner?" Turning to Iko, he whispered, "Are you sure you're all right? You're very pale."

"I'll be fine," said Iko.

"I asked if you *are* fine, not if you *will be* fine." He glanced around, as though checking none of the men were within earshot. "If they think you're not well, they might think you're going to lose control of the dragon."

Iko tried to stand straight and nearly fell over. The deck was swaying too much — no, that was his head. "I think," he began, and then paused, unsure of what he thought. "I think I need to lean on you."

Serl draped Iko's uninjured arm over his shoulders and slipped an arm around Iko's waist. Iko felt safe and warm. His eyelids drooped — he could fall asleep here.

A distant voice reached him. Something jabbed him in the ribs.

"Ow!"

"The hoist is ready," Serl said.

The pirates had rigged a complicated arrangement of ropes around Esald's leg on either side of the wound. The men were all looking at him expectantly. What did they need him for?

"Do we lift?" Serl whispered.

"What? Yes, I suppose so."

The pirates heaved on ropes that hung from spars on the foremast. Fresh pain shredded Iko's arm, and he screamed. The pirates stopped pulling.

"What's going on?" said the leader. "If we're hurting the monster, how come he's the one bawling?"

Shivering, Iko tried to speak. Words wouldn't come.

"The control works both ways," said Serl. "When the dragon gets hurt, he feels some of its pain."

"So if we kill him, does that mean the dragon dies too?"

Without missing a beat, Serl replied, "No, it means the dragon won't be under his control any more. Why do you think he didn't try to eat anyone when you went climbing all over him?"

The leader shrugged, and nodded to the other men, who resumed pulling on the ropes. The pain in Iko's arm returned, worse than before. Serl, perhaps sensing what was about to happen, clapped a hand over Iko's mouth. The stump of the mast glistened as more blood oozed from the wound.

At last, the leg was free of the stump, and a couple of the pirates pushed it clear before their comrades released the ropes. Iko felt himself sliding free of Serl's support. There was no pain as he hit the deck. He heard Serl say, "Bind the wound," before darkness claimed him.

Chapter 13

Iko woke to find himself on the shore. Serl knelt by him, pressing a damp cloth to his forehead. He sat up, waving Serl away. Without thinking, Iko put his weight on the "injured" arm and cried out as renewed pain shot through it. On the bright side, that meant Esald was still alive. But it also meant the dragon wasn't going anywhere soon.

The pirate chief, who'd been standing with a group of his men near the wrecked ship, strolled over to Iko and Serl.

"So," he said, resting a hand on his sword hilt, "we did as ye asked, and the beast's still here."

Iko looked past the group to see a dark shape sprawled over the ship. "Yes, well." He coughed — his voice seemed rusty from disuse. "He, ah, took a terrible wound. Dragons heal faster than humans, but you can hardly expect him to fly away so soon."

"I gave ye until the ebb tide. That's an hour away." He returned to the group.

It had been six hours to ebb tide when Iko started this mad scheme. He'd been unconscious for much longer than he thought.

"What now?" said Serl.

Iko held out a hand, and Serl pulled him to his feet. "We need to see Esald," Iko said.

The ship had sunk lower, to the point that the gangplank sloped down from the wharf. Esald's head still drooped over the side, now less than a foot from the water. Could a dragon drown? Iko didn't want to find out. The wound had been bandaged, apparently with fabric cut from the sails, but already the lower half of the bandage was soaked with blood.

Esald, Iko said with his mind. *Can you hear me? We need to leave. Do you think you might be able to fly?*

The dragon's head lifted a fraction, and his eyelids fluttered. *Your supply of inane questions never ceases to amaze me.*

Praise Mazor! I persuaded the pirates to take the mast out of your leg, but we need to leave within the hour.

I suppose that is your idea of mercy, Esald said. *If you want to show mercy, drive a spear through my eye socket. At the right angle, it will enter my brain. Death will be instant.*

How can you say such things? Iko shuddered. *You told me dragons heal quickly.*

I can — and have — survived injuries that would kill you. But I am not immortal.

"What's he saying?" Serl asked.

Turning to face Serl, Iko gulped. "He wants us to kill him."

"You did tell him that his obligation to you isn't complete?"

"I… I was just going to do that." To Esald, Iko said, *You have not fulfilled your promise to me, dragon. The pirates agreed to leave my people alone if you were gone from here by the ebb tide, which is an hour away.*

I am not party to agreements you make with these pirates, human.

Then I am telling you that as a condition of fulfilling your promise to me, you need to leave here within the hour.

I will not be capable of flight within that time. I will not even be able to walk.

Iko screwed his eyes shut. *If you die here, we cannot stop the pirates from continuing to raid my home! All our efforts will have been for nothing!*

I promised I would do my utmost, said Esald. *I did not promise I would succeed.*

Iko told Serl what the dragon had said. Serl was silent for several moments, then replied, "You said he could cross between our world and theirs."

"Yes, but he has to be flying," said Iko.

"It's worth a try, surely? It would show your control over him — make him disappear before their eyes."

With a sigh, Iko said to Esald, *Can you cross over into the dragons' world?*

Do you not think I would have done so as soon as I realised I was impaled?

You are not impaled any longer, Iko said.

It is extremely dangerous to cross between worlds when not in the air.

A slim chance of survival is better than none.

Perhaps you are right. Stand back. There is likely to be an explosion.

Iko started towards the shore. Serl clapped a hand on his shoulder.

"What are you doing?"

"He's going to try to cross over. He wants us to stand further away."

Serl pulled Iko towards the gangplank. "If he's leaving, we have to go with him."

"It's dangerous. There could be an explosion."

Leaning in, Serl whispered, "If we're still here when he's gone, I'd give it two minutes before the pirates slit our throats."

Iko looked over his shoulder. The chief was still standing on the shore, conferring with his henchmen. "What about your boat?" Iko whispered back.

"We'll just have to leave it. With a bit of luck, the tide will drag it out to sea before this lot find it."

Iko nodded. *We're coming with you,* he said to Esald.

You are likely to die, Esald replied.

I survived two crossings before.

Not when I was near to death.

Iko said, *If we stay here, the pirates will kill us as soon as you're gone.*

Two slim chances instead of one. Very well, then.

Iko waved to the chief.

"What?" the man called.

"We're leaving now, with the dragon. You might want to retreat to a safe distance."

The man scowled. "What's yer idea of a 'safe distance?'"

"A few hundred yards, maybe."

"All right. Don't think it'll save ye if yer planning anything tricky, mind."

"Remember your promise," Iko said as the pirates started walking along the beach. "You leave the Lenis Islands alone."

"Oh, I'll remember," the chief said over his shoulder. "Ye can be sure of that."

"Notice he didn't say he'd *keep* the promise," Serl muttered as they boarded the ship.

"Nothing we can do about that now," Iko replied.

Climb onto my back, Esald said, *and find something to hold on to.* His back was much too broad to sit astride, so they lay flat on it, between the wings, and each gripped one of the spikes that ran along his spine.

We're ready, Iko said.

The dragon's muscles bunched and tensed, and for a moment, Iko thought he was preparing to throw them off. Esald relaxed, then tensed again. His wings lifted fractionally. The edges of Iko's vision went purple.

"What's that?" Serl said, looking around.

Before Iko could shush him, there was a deafening crash. Something sharp struck Iko's leg. Wind slapped him from above and both sides. His stomach lurched, and he felt himself falling. Before panic could take hold, there was a loud splash. Everything tilted forward, then back, and a wave of warm water sloshed over him.

Chapter 14

"Is it safe to breathe again?" Serl whispered.

Iko looked up. For as far as he could see, there was nothing but sky and ocean. Both had a purple cast. "He did it. He crossed over to the dragons' world."

"So what happens now?"

Esald lay motionless on the ship, or what was left of it. The masts had gone, as had the forecastle, and the doorway and windows in the front of the poop deck looked onto open air. The deck lay even closer to the water than in the pirates' harbour. Iko slid down from Esald's back. The timbers flexed under his feet. The port side, where Esald's head hung over into the sea, was already awash. Rope lay in tangles everywhere, along with chunks of wood like the chippings left behind when a man cut down a tree. Serl clambered over Esald's spikes and climbed down to stand near Iko.

"He ripped the deck off the ship when he crossed over," said Iko. "That must be why he said it was dangerous — ropes and splinters whizzing around."

Serl pointed to Iko's leg. "You're bleeding."

Blood trickled from an inch-long cut. "I thought something hit me. It doesn't hurt." Only now did he notice that his upper arm had stopped hurting too.

The binding is broken, said Esald. *I have completed my task.*

Iko turned to look at the bandages on Esald's leg. *Your bleeding seems to have stopped.*

I have no more blood to give. Death will come soon.

What about us? said Iko. *I know that's a horrible thing to say at a time like this, but if you die, we'll be stranded here.*

79

That is regrettable, said Esald, *but you did say you would prefer our world to yours, given the circumstances.*

I did. I thank you for saving us from the pirates. To Serl, he said, "The dragon's dying."

"That's been obvious for a while," Serl muttered.

What do dragons believe happens to them after they die? said Iko.

That is one of many things we do not discuss with people who are not dragons. Iko noted that he'd graduated from *man-thing* to *human* and finally to *person.*

I thank you for battling the pirates, said Iko, *and for letting me see your world. Flight is wonderful. Terrifying, but wonderful.*

Esald did not answer, and Iko thought he might have died already. Then, *I thank you for showing me that my understanding of your kind was... incomplete.*

The dragon did not speak again.

Iko stared out over the sea, not knowing what he was looking for. He fought a silent struggle against the tears that threatened to overcome him. He thought of Mother, sitting on the wharf, staring out to sea for the rest of her days. He should've done more to look after her as she grew older, especially after Father died.

Murmurs came from the left. He turned to see Serl speaking, lips barely moving.

"He told me our Gods don't watch over them," Iko said.

"My father once told me the prayers for the departed are more for the benefit of those left behind than those who've gone."

Iko felt a dampness in the corner of one eye. "Then he was wiser than many of my colleagues at the monastery." He laid a hand on the dragon's flank. Together, he and Serl recited the prayers that committed a soul to the care of Mazor and Kashalbe. By the time they were done, Iko's face was wet, and his throat felt like stone.

Serl looked down and grimaced. Iko followed his gaze to see water lapping at their shoes.

"We could use what's left of the deck as a raft if we could

move him off it," Serl said.

"We're not going to be able to move him," Iko replied.

"Then we'll have to climb on top of him. We might be able to slide the deck out from under him once he's sunk enough."

"That's disrespectful."

"It's not as if he's going to object."

So they clambered on top of the dragon's body, even as it sank inch by inch below the waves.

"You do realise, of course," said Iko, "that this is only delaying the inevitable."

"Being alive is delaying the inevitable," Serl replied.

"Well, yes," said Iko, "but even if we make a raft, we've got no way of moving it, no food or water, and no way of crossing back to the human world."

"Even if we could get back, we wouldn't want to — the pirates would kill us. But if we could move the raft and then cross over…"

"We could drown or die of thirst there instead of here," Iko said.

"How does that work, anyway? The crossing over, I mean."

"I haven't the faintest idea."

"You need a dragon, then," Serl said. "A live one, that is."

Iko shrugged — an awkward gesture when he was lying down. "Presumably."

"So couldn't you summon one?"

"The spell doesn't actually summon a dragon," said Iko. "It just tells any dragons in the vicinity that you'd like them to come to you."

"That must be why it took him so long to show up after you cast the spell — he had to fly to us from wherever he was. But you might as well try it now. What's the worst that could happen?"

"They could kill us for our impertinence, the way Esald nearly did the first time I met him."

"And would that be worse than drowning or dying of thirst?" said Serl.

"They're very intelligent, and they've had a long time to nurse a hatred of humans," said Iko. "They might decide to kill us slowly."

"More slowly than the pirates would?"

"Maybe not." He took a breath and recited the spell.

Several moments passed. Serl looked up, squinting, then rose to his feet, wobbling as Esald's body and the ship's deck pitched under him. "That was quick." He pointed to the horizon. Iko shaded his eyes with his hand. A gnat-sized dot hung in the sky, wavering in the haze.

Serl waved his arms, then pulled off his shirt and swung it round like a flag. He stopped and stared again. "It's coming this way."

"I don't think I did that, actually..."

Serl resumed waving. "There's two of them."

"I definitely didn't do that."

As the dots drew nearer, they resolved into two dragons — one black, one red. Their voices rang in Iko's head, crying, *Esald, Esald!*

Esald is dead! Iko called back to them.

Alas! said one of the dragons. *We feared this was so.* They flew around Esald's body in a broad circle, soaring and diving, low enough that the tips of their wings clipped the water. A terrible howling came from them, mind and voice alike.

Serl clapped his hands over his ears. "What are they *doing?*"

"Isn't it obvious?"

"If it was, I wouldn't have asked."

"Grieving."

The humans must have killed him, said one of the dragons.

No! Iko shouted.

The human that bound him is still alive, said the other dragon. They flew further apart now, and Iko could tell the red one had spoken that time. *He must have completed the task the human set for him.*

Then the human must have killed him after that, once the binding had dissolved, the black dragon said.

Esald's distress call made no mention of being murdered, said the red dragon. Now Iko recognised their voices — they were two of the dragons in the conclave that Esald had taken him to. The red one was Athera, and the black one Vadim — the most hostile of the three. Iko wondered why he hadn't heard anything he could describe as a distress call.

We must take his body back to Sarn Kathakhdim, said Vadim.

A ridiculous superstition, said Athera.

Vadim flew nearer to Athera, low enough for Iko to feel the downdraught from his wings, and snapped his jaws. *Do not let the others hear you say that.*

The two of us cannot lift him. By the time others have arrived, he will have sunk beneath the waves.

Vadim snapped his jaws again. *Then the last person to see him alive must go.*

Iko tried to swallow past a fist-sized lump in his throat. *That would be me.* He glanced at Serl. *Us.*

Ridiculous, Vadim growled.

But evidently true, Athera replied. To Iko, he said, *Stand apart from the other human, so that I can lift you up.*

Iko stood straighter. *If I go, he comes with me.*

I did not say otherwise, the dragon replied. *But each of us can carry only one of you.*

Then take him first, Iko said.

You do not trust us.

Not as much as you seem to want me to.

Very well, Athera said. *I will take him.*

"What are they saying?" Serl said.

"They want to take us with them, to, I think, attend some kind of funeral service for Esald. Stand as far from me as you can. The red one is going to pick you up."

"What?" Serl looked around wildly, as though trying to decide where to run for cover.

"Just do as I say."

At Athera's instruction, Serl stood on the highest point of Esald's back. Iko lay down, near Esald's hind legs. Athera retreated to a distance and height where he was little more than a dot. Vadim continued to circle. Athera approached Serl from behind. He slowed down as he came nearer, wings spread wide. When he was within a few body lengths of Serl, he raised his front half and stretched out his front legs as though about to embrace a lover. He tilted his wings, slowing to the point where he seemed to hang motionless. Wind whipped at Serl's clothes and hair. Then the dragon's legs closed around him. Athera's tail slapped the water and his wings pumped, carrying them aloft.

To Serl's credit, he didn't scream until the dragon had gained enough height to start levelling out.

Iko stood, hearing the slow, steady *whoomph, whoomph* of Vadim's wings behind him. The wind nearly knocked him over, but he remained standing long enough for the dragon to grab him. The dragon bore him aloft, much faster and rougher than Esald ever had. They settled a few hundred yards behind Athera and Serl.

Vadim's voice slipped into Iko's mind like a burglar sneaking through a back door. *Were I to let you fall, man-thing, no one would know you did not slip from my claws.*

Iko tried to keep his own mental voice steady. *Except that I would scream your treachery as loud as I could. And the other human cannot speak to dragons, so you need me alive.*

You assume much to think that we need either of you alive.

Then why take the trouble of lifting us from the sea? said Iko.

Cruelty was one of many things we learned from you during our enslavement, the dragon replied.

Chapter 15

They flew on in silence for a couple of hours before a black, spiky island came into view, like Esald's home but much larger. Dozens of dragons, of all colours and sizes, circled it, hooting and howling their grief.

Athera and Vadim drew near to a large square of muddy ground, about halfway up the island. *Are we going to land there?* said Iko.

Yes, replied Vadim.

"Serl!" Iko shouted. "We're about to land! The dragon will throw you clear! When he does, curl into a ball so you roll when you hit the ground!"

Serl gave no sign he had heard. The dragons descended together, coming in only a few yards above the square. Involuntarily, Iko shut his eyes at the sight of the ground rushing up to meet him, then forced them open. Vadim flicked him free, as though skimming a stone across a pond. His stomach fell, and just in time, he remembered his advice to Serl, drawing his knees up to his chest and tucking his head between them.

He hit the ground with a wet thud, then half-rolled, half-slid to a stop. Shaking, he stood up. He judged he'd have a few bruises, but nothing like when Esald had dropped him. He was getting better at this. Or maybe it was just that this ground was softer than anything Esald had dropped him on.

Serl lay a few yards away, groaning. Iko helped him to his feet, saying, "Did you not hear me say to curl into a ball?"

Wincing, Serl rubbed his back. "I did. I just didn't think the dragon would actually throw me."

It seemed unnaturally quiet, and Iko took a moment to

realise that the dragons had stopped howling. They crowded nearer to the square, studying the new arrivals.

Athera and Vadim had circled round and were now landing. A few more followed, mainly drab green with one iridescent blue. A fluttering made Iko look round. More green dragons had landed behind him and Serl, meaning they were now surrounded.

Seeing the fear on Serl's face, Iko murmured, "If they were going to kill us, they could've done it already."

"Maybe they want to do it publicly," Serl replied. "They look to be a lot more organised than I thought at first."

Another black dragon landed near the edge of the square. Iko guessed this had to be Kelekh, the third dragon who had been at the conclave with Athera and Vadim.

Man-things, said Athera, strutting towards them, wings held above his body, half-extended. *You will tell us of Esald's deeds, beginning with his last crossing to your world and ending with his death.*

And then what? said Iko.

What do you mean, "And then what?" said Athera.

Will you send us back to our world?

For a moment, the dragon did not answer. Then, *That depends on what you have to say about Esald. We will know if you lie.*

I understand, Iko replied. *The other human saw some things I did not, but he cannot speak as dragons do. I will speak for him.*

As you wish.

There was much that neither of us saw. The pirates held us prisoner until after Esald arrived.

Then tell us what you did see, said the dragon.

So Iko told them what had happened, beginning with when he had tried to summon Esald on the cliff overlooking the pirates' harbour and ending with Athera and Vadim's arrival at the site of Esald's death. The dragons let him talk without interruption, and he was quite exhausted when he'd finished — this was by far the longest amount of time he'd spent speaking in the dragons' fashion.

And is that everything that happened? asked Athera.

Yes, Iko replied.

Now Esald can go with pride into the next world, said the dragon. *We must consider what you have told us.* Some of the dragons at the edge of the gathering drifted away, howling faintly. Kelekh came to join Athera and Vadim. He flapped his wings as he did so, half-walking, half-hopping. The three dragons turned to face one another. Iko heard no speech, but instead a noise that at times resembled birdsong and at other times a group of beehives.

"What are they doing?" Serl whispered.

"Deciding what to do with us, I think," said Iko.

"So this is a trial, then. That explains why they didn't kill us right away."

The dragons turned to look at the humans. *We have reached a decision,* said Athera. The answer must have been obvious if it was so quick. *We hold you partly responsible for Esald's death, as you bound him.*

Iko gulped. *He agreed to be bound. Perhaps not consciously —*

The dragon cut him off with, *Be quiet. Admittedly, that is why we hold you only partly responsible. He was foolish beyond his years. Against that, we must weigh the fact that you helped him to return to our world to die, together with the deaths of — well, we do not know the exact number, but we will accept your figure of a hundred — a hundred of these "pirates".*

I didn't want to kill any of them, said Iko.

What you wanted is irrelevant. The question for us to settle was, is the death of a hundred humans worth the death of one dragon?

May Kashalbe forgive you, Iko whispered. *No life is more valuable than any other.*

Your Gods do not watch over us, the dragon said. *We hold a hundred lives of your kind a fair payment for one of ours. Therefore we will return you to your world.*

Iko let go of a breath. *Thank you, o great dragon.*

We will return you to your world as a warning to others of your kind who might think to meddle in our affairs.

Do you mean to kill us, then?

We killed untold numbers of your kind during the Liberation, said Athera, *and still you would not leave our world alone. Obviously that is not the answer. It is time to try something new. Mount on my back, both of you.*

The two humans did as the dragon said. The other dragons cleared a path in front of him, and he charged towards the edge of the square. Iko shuddered as the dragon's feet slipped in the mud, but they were soon airborne.

After perhaps ten minutes, Athera said, *I heard Vadim's threat to drop you into the sea. Most likely he was merely attempting to frighten you, but I have to take it seriously.*

Thank you, said Iko.

I do not need your gratitude, the dragon replied. He did not speak again until another spiky island came into view. *I am about to cross to your world. Hold tight. I have not practiced this as much as Esald did.*

As Iko was relaying this to Serl, a purple flash blinded him for a moment. Athera dropped several feet and tilted sideways before resuming stable flight. The island had been replaced with a larger and less precipitous one.

"That's home," Serl said. Iko hadn't recognised it at first, never having seen it from this angle.

Athera landed smoothly on Ansrad Hill. As soon as Iko and Serl had dismounted and were clear of him, he said *Do not attempt to summon us again,* and took off again.

They started down the hill, and then Serl said, "The path is on this side, isn't it?"

"Yes," said Iko.

"Where is it, then?"

Where Iko thought he remembered the path being was badly overgrown. They found another route down, threading their way among scraggly trees that grew on the side facing the sea.

When the village came into view, Serl put out his arm to stop Iko and said, "Something's wrong." He pointed to the shore. "There are four docks. We've only got two. And you see those houses along the road to Samdurath? They shouldn't be there."

"Maybe the dragon brought us to the wrong island," said Iko. Even as the words left his mouth, he knew that wasn't likely — too many other things were as he remembered them. "Or maybe... you remember when Esald brought me back, I thought I'd been gone for a few hours, and I'd really been gone for a week and a half?"

Serl nodded slowly, looking as though he'd swallowed a mouthful of sour milk.

"So maybe we've been gone much longer this time."

"How much longer?"

"I don't know. We'll just have to find someone and ask them." As they started walking again, Iko added, "Let's see if we can get into the monastery without anyone in the village seeing us. My colleagues might be a little more accepting of the fact we're reappearing after a long absence."

They cut across the fields inland of the village and circled around to come to the front of the monastery. The gate stood half-open. Weeds grew between the gaps in the flagstones. As they entered, Iko saw a large lump of stone that had fallen from a wall, smashing the flags underneath it. Ivy clung to the buildings, and several shutters on the lower floors were missing.

"I'd say the place is abandoned," said Serl. "Let's see if we can find someone in the village."

As they turned to leave, a voice called, "Hello?" An old woman came around a corner and shuffled towards them. She wore the clothes of a permanent monk, albeit much frayed and patched. She stopped after a few paces and shaded her eyes with a hand. "How may I help you?"

"Greetings, Sister," Iko began.

"It's been a long time since anyone called me that," the woman said.

"We, ah, we used to live here some years ago," Iko said. "We're passing through on our way to somewhere else, and we wondered if anyone we knew was still here. Is there someone in charge we could speak to?"

"I suppose I'm..." She paused and raised a finger. "I know

your voice." She took a few more paces and squinted. "Teacher Iko?"

Iko gasped. "How do you know me?"

"Don't you remember me? Sister Drubath?"

"I remember you, but Gods, what happened to you?"

Drubath cackled. "What happened? I got old, and everyone else left. Some of the villagers still check on me from time to time, to be sure I haven't died." She came closer. "You look too young to be Iko. Are you his son?"

Iko shook his head. "We went to find the pirates' base." He indicated Serl and himself. "We were going to summon the dragon there to frighten them into leaving us alone."

"Pirates?" Drubath frowned. "We haven't had any trouble with them since..." She put a hand to her mouth. "Oh Gods. You never came back, but the pirate attacks stopped. We assumed your boat sunk, or the pirates killed you. So your plan actually worked?"

"Don't sound so surprised," said Serl.

"Serl?" said Drubath, seeming to notice him for the first time.

"How long have we been gone?" said Serl.

Drubath frowned and gazed into the distance. "Twenty... no, thirty-one years. Or is it thirty-two?"

"Gods," Serl whispered.

Emptiness yawned inside Iko. He'd thought they would've been gone a couple of months — a year or two at most. "My mother," he croaked.

"Dead," Drubath replied.

Iko staggered backwards, as if he'd been kicked in the stomach. Serl laid a hand on his shoulder and scowled at Drubath.

"Why are you so surprised?" Drubath asked. "She was nearly sixty."

Iko did a quick calculation in his head. "Twenty years ago."

Drubath shrugged. "About that."

"How's that possible?" Serl asked. "You saw her, what — ten days past?"

Iko dabbed at his eyes. He'd known Mother couldn't have

been expected to live much longer, but he'd always thought he'd have the chance to say goodbye to her.

Drubath squinted at them again. "Are you sure you're Iko and Serl? You look as though you'd have been suckling when the pirates were bothering us."

"It's us," said Iko. "The dragon took us into his world to escape them, and time passes faster there than here. What happened to the monastery? Where's everyone else?"

"Closed. The Proctor died unexpectedly, and there was a big argument over the succession, and then some 'irregularities' were found in the accounts, and it turned out we owed a lot of money, and to pay it off, we had to sell most of the books in the library."

"No," Iko breathed.

"The books about dragons are still here," said Drubath. "Nobody seemed to want them."

"That's no consolation," said Iko.

"Most of the monks and some of the teachers moved to neighbouring monasteries. A few stayed in the village, though it's been years since I've seen them."

Iko sat on the ground with a thump and buried his face in his hands. After a few moments, he looked up at Drubath, sight blurred. "That scroll you found for me — it warned me something like this might happen. The dragons gave me what I wanted, but I don't think it was worth what it cost me."

Serl rested a hand on Iko's shoulder. "I wasn't going to tell you this unless you — unless I thought you weren't willing to go through with everything."

Iko twisted to look at him.

"A couple of the settlements further up the coast — if the raids didn't stop, they were going to abandon their homes and move inland."

"I'd no idea the situation was that desperate," Iko replied. "And if they had left, the pirates would've taken even more from the settlements that were still occupied."

Serl nodded and stood up straight. "So, what now?"

"What do you mean?"

"How do we get home?"

"This is home," Iko said.

"No, I mean how do we get to — to..." Serl waved his hands, evidently lacking the words he needed.

"Back to our own time? Thirty-one years ago?" He sighed. "We can't."

Serl stared at him. "How do you know? The dragon brought us here, he can —" He paused, perhaps stopped from swearing by Drubath's presence.

Iko shook his head. "I don't know for sure that there's no way back. But it seems obvious that if there is a way, it must involve the dragons."

"So what's the problem? Summon that red one, we'll share a flagon of wine and have a laugh at the joke he played on us, and we can all go back to how we were this morning."

"I don't think he meant this as a joke," Iko said. "Before we left the island, he told me they were going to try a new way to make us leave them alone. And when he took off just now, he warned me not to summon them again."

Serl frowned. "What'll they do if you try?"

"He didn't say, but it's not hard to guess, is it?"

"They'll kill you?"

Iko nodded. "You too, I imagine."

"And is that worse than..." Serl tailed off, glancing at Drubath.

"Spending the rest of our lives here?" Iko stood up, knees protesting. "There's only one way to find out. It wouldn't have been my first choice, but we've been stuck in much less pleasant places." He motioned Serl and Drubath to follow him, and the three of them headed for the main gate. "Let's see if anyone else remembers their saviours, shall we?"

Acknowledgements

I would like to thank the following people for their help in bringing this book to you —

- My partner Breda for her love and understanding.
- My family for their support and encouragement.
- My critique partners Terry Odell and Karla Brandenburg for reading the early drafts.
- The readers of the final draft, for pointing out plot holes and continuity errors — in no particular order, Ciaran Quirke, Paul Fitzjohn, Rachel Cotterill, Calico J Maher, Breda and my mother Joyce.

If you enjoyed this book, please tell your friends about it, and please consider leaving a review on the site where you bought it. Thank you.

If you'd like to be the first to know when I release a new book, you can subscribe to my mailing list by going to www.pembers.net and clicking the "Mailing List" link at the bottom of the page.

About the Author

I was born in England in 1970, the son of a librarian and a teacher. It was probably inevitable, therefore, that I would grow up loving books. For most of my childhood, my family and I lived in New Zealand, returning to England in 1981. I graduated from the University of York in 1992 with a bachelor's degree in computer science. I now live in Hertfordshire with my partner, where I work as a software developer.

Visit my website at www.pembers.net for bonus material for this book and news of forthcoming releases.

Printed in Great Britain
by Amazon

28466031R00056